That One Small Omission

Willow River Press is an imprint of Between the Lines Publishing. The Willow River Press name and logo are trademarks of Between the Lines Publishing.

Between the Lines Publishing
1769 Lexington Ave N, Ste 286
Roseville MN 55113
btwnthelines.com

First Published: November 2025

ISBN: (Paperback) 978-1-965059-69-2

ISBN: (eBook) 978-1-965059-70-8

That One Small Omission

Kris Francoeur

For Paul, the love of my life, and for Sam who
still serves as a guiding light.

Chapter One

Devon tilted his head. "You got reprimanded?"

Maggie sighed, "Yeah, a formal verbal reprimand. And was told I'm lucky it wasn't a formal *written* reprimand that would go in my personnel file."

"I don't get it. Why were you reprimanded?" Mike asked, as he poured more merlot into all three glasses.

Devon smiled, then asked, "Mags, start again. Start to finish, what happened today with the Dean and President?"

Maggie stiffened. "Stop sounding like a lawyer."

"I *am* a lawyer. And knowing you, I may have to defend you in a labor lawsuit at some point, so I want to make sure I have my facts straight."

Maggie took a sip of wine. "It's a long story."

Devon looked at Mike, who shrugged, "We've got time."

She smiled, "Does it ever occur to the two of you that our social lives suck? That *this* is the extent of our social lives?"

Mike chuckled, "You mean that after almost twenty years of friendship, our big social event is getting together every month to eat pizza and drink wine?"

Devon's eyes clouded with sadness, "It used to be the four of us."

Maggie squeezed his hand, "And she specifically told us she'd come back to haunt us if we didn't continue the tradition."

Devon continued, "True. Now explain what happened."

"Oh, the whole day sucked. It started badly…"

The day *had* started badly. Maggie awoke in a fog, smelling coffee. She usually woke early to work out, her coffee pot set to start automatically while she showered. Smelling coffee clearly meant she was already running at least an hour behind. Damn!

Twenty minutes later, she poured the java into a travel mug. As she stepped over the toys scattered across the rug, her heart constricted. It always felt so weird when the boys were away. At least this morning, she could probably still make her meeting relatively on time since she wouldn't have to stop at daycare.

Five minutes later, she pulled into the lot and grimaced to see another car occupying her normal spot. After three futile circuits, she finally pulled onto the grass at the side of the lot, hoping Security would ignore her car this one time.

She hopped out of the car and yanked her bag from the passenger seat, breaking into a jog toward the Commons Building. How could she be late for the most important faculty meeting of the year? With luck, she could duck in the back door and find a seat without anyone noticing.

No such luck. The open door cast a spear of sunlight across the otherwise dark room, prompting most of the audience to turn and stare back at her. Dean Anderson smiled smugly from the podium next to the overhead of the projected budget for the next year. "Nice of you to join us, Ms. Erickson."

Her face burning, Maggie slid into the nearest empty seat, wishing she had managed to be there twenty-five minutes earlier, at the start of the meeting.

At the end of the meeting, the Dean raised his hand to signal for attention. "I hope you all have a happy and relaxing spring break, and we'll see you all next week.

Please remember to check your email for faculty updates. And, Ms. Erickson, I'd like a word with you."

Maggie stood warily, her stomach churning in anger. In the back of the room, her two assistants and two classroom teachers waited, silently lending their support.

Anderson smoothed a wrinkle from the sleeve of his navy-blue blazer. "I appreciate you bothering to show up for this meeting. After all, you referred to it yesterday in the snack bar, as, I believe, 'the biggest waste of time' since you took the oral exam for my South African history class. However, it would have shown a minimum of professional courtesy on your part had you arrived on time."

Before Maggie could answer, he continued. "While I realize you believe it is acceptable for your staff to be a bit lackadaisical, *I* expect when I call a meeting, you will arrive on time."

Swallowing, Maggie tried to keep calm. "Sir, I certainly intended to be here for the start of the meeting; my alarm didn't go off. I got here as soon as I could."

He snorted. "And what was the excuse for missing the meeting last month? I believe you had a sick child who kept you from your professional obligations." Tipping his head slightly, he raised one eyebrow. "I find it fascinating how often your children are sick on faculty meeting days."

Maggie struggled to keep her voice low and calm "I have never missed a meeting without a good reason."

He stroked his long, graying handlebar mustache carefully, a mannerism Maggie had always hated. "It's certainly regrettable that you missed the start of the meeting. I announced an adjustment to your program. Beginning in the fall, you will have student teachers for six weeks, rather than twelve. This will mean we can offer endorsements in Special Education for twice as many students."

"What? That means the students, I mean the high school students, will have to adjust to twice as many staff, and you know they can't handle a transition like that. You *know* that." Maggie's cheeks colored with her rising voice.

"Frankly, it's not my business how well they adjust, that's your job to handle. My concern is how many college students earn the endorsement, increasing the viability of the Teacher Education program."

"Sir, with all due respect, if those students don't adjust to the changes in staff, your future teachers won't stay in a classroom; they'll leave running and screaming."

"Then you'll have to make sure that doesn't happen. If you can't serve the best interests of the college students, perhaps you need to think about another line of work. Or at least another *place* of work." He smiled, his eyes narrowing. "It was my decision to make this change. It's in the best interests of the college. *Your* function is to work with your staff to make sure it happens well."

Ever since she was a baby-faced freshman of eighteen, Maggie struggled to bite her tongue when Dean Anderson belittled her. For the last four years of meetings and appointments, she managed to stay cool under his disdainful eye, but she couldn't take it anymore. She snapped. "Oh, bite me!"

His voice rose to a mosquito-like whine. "Did you just say, 'bite me'?"

"Yes, I did, you sanctimonious piece of shit. How dare you insinuate I don't care about this college, or that I won't do my job to the best of my ability?"

"Excuse me? Did you just curse at me? I guess I'm not surprised; belligerence is exactly what I'd expect from someone who works with the type of children you do."

"You asshole. *That's* what this is about. I work with kids you think should be marginalized, and you can't stand it. Aren't you the one who once told our state representative that only college-educated people should be allowed to vote? You hate the fact that the program works, and the college could actually be seen as welcoming to someone outside of the affluent, blond elite."

"Ms. Erickson, your obscene mouth and gross insubordination will be reported, and you can expect the appropriate sanctions to soon follow."

Maggie was beyond caring. "Whatever blows your skirt up, Anderson," she said and peevishly spun on her heel.

Back in the kitchen, Maggie grimaced, "And that is how my day went."

The two men sat across the table regarding her silently. Sipping his wine, Mike swallowed before saying, "I guess you're not up for Employee of the Year anymore. Do you still have a job?"

"Yeah, I still have a job, but about an hour later I got a call from Priscilla."

Devon's face lit up, "How is she? I loved working for her!"

"Priscilla's fine, but she called and said I needed to be in the President's office in fifteen minutes. I had to jog across campus to get there in time. I figured the Dean would be there too, but when I got there, I was just meeting with the President."

"And?"

"He sat me down, looked at me, and gave the biggest sigh I ever heard. Then he told me I was frustrating the hell out of him; that he loves me, he loves what I bring to the college, and he loves the program, but we were meeting in private, so he didn't have to worry about being politically correct. He told me flat-out that I'm a pain in the ass."

Mike nodded, "True."

Maggie glared, not finding the humor, "That I am wholeheartedly devoted to my students, both the college students, and our clients."

Devon nodded, "Also true."

"That I have great trouble accepting authority, which he finds interesting, since I grew up in a military family."

Before either man responded, Maggie snapped, "I know, *true*. Then he said that no matter how much he loves me and wants me at the college, I have to learn to get along with the Dean, period. He said the severity of this incident would normally mean I'd receive a formal written reprimand, but since it was the first time it rose to this level, he was giving me a verbal warning telling me I need to get my shit together and stop reacting to Anderson."

Devon queried, "Is he noting the verbal warning in your personnel file?"

"No, as long as I don't have another issue this school year, it's done. If I tell him off again, it'll be noted in the file and then I'll get written up. Mind passing the merlot?"

"You got off easy, you know that, right?" Devon said, passing her the bottle.

She sighed, "Yeah, I know. If Jason wasn't the President, I'd be screwed right now. The two of you would be helping me update my resume."

"I have to say, overall, that ended better than it could have. What about the rest of the day?"

Shaking her head, Maggie continued. "My mother called four times to tell me everything I forgot to send with the boys, as if the world would stop turning if they didn't have their own toothpaste. Couldn't they use hers? It *really* helped to have her remind me today that on top of everything else, she thinks I'm a shitty mother. And just in case I wasn't already looking to punch somebody, I got a parking ticket from Campus Security."

Maggie rolled her eyes as she picked an olive off her pizza, pausing a moment before flicking it into the empty box. "And I *told* them no olives because I really didn't need any fucking olives today. All in all, the day sucked." She flicked another olive, "But I forgot to tell you the best part of my meeting with the President."

"What's that?"

She lowered her eyes, not wanting to see their immediate reactions. "I get to attend five anger management sessions with a therapist; starting tomorrow night."

Both men struggled to keep straight faces, but their belly laughs soon filled the kitchen.

Chapter Two

Maggie drove home the next night in a funk after her first therapy session. In her living room, she looked at the assignment sheet and grimaced: "*Welcome to Anger Management Therapy – Dr. Charles (Charlie) Robinson, Ph.D., Therapist. While attending these sessions, you are required to keep a daily personal journal, which will have a combination of questions to guide you in your individual quest, as well as provide room for personal sharing and reflection. We will be reviewing the journal at each session, and, if you are comfortable doing so, please feel free to share any additional personal experiences. Remember, our goal is to help you overcome your tendency to let anger rule your life – not to judge you on your life choices.*"

Maggie rolled her eyes, "Bullshit," she said, then continued reading. "<u>First Assignment:</u> *Who are you? Why are you here? Do you feel you should be here? What are the top five things that make you angry?*"

"Filling out this fucking journal is top on my list of things that piss me off right now," Maggie said, and reached for an Oreo. *I'm Maggie Erickson-O'Brien, thirty-four years old, teacher and college professor. I have two sons, Eli (5) and Nick (3), who are absolutely amazing. I pretty much raise them alone because my ex-husband is an Air Force pilot.*

Her pencil lead snapped. Annoyed, she pulled another from the cup next to the phone. "This is worse than college application essays."

I have two older brothers. Carl is a doctor, and Neil is in the military. I also have two sisters. Kim is my older sister, a corporate headhunter in Montreal, and my younger sister Jessie is twenty-two, currently in Tibet, "finding herself."

I'm here because I seem to have offended my supervisor when I publicly called him a few choice words. As a consequence, the college is making me attend therapy. I'm trying to convince myself it's probably better to attend these sessions than lose my job.

The top five things that irritate or make me angry: nonsense meetings, useless paperwork (busywork, as I see it), drivers who meander down the road below the speed limit, my bra strap slipping down my shoulders when I'm in a professional setting, and my mother insinuating I'm not a good parent.

Chapter Three

Droopy, damp, and tired.

The next afternoon, Maggie's khaki capris and white blouse were soaked from the rain, her blouse sticking to her body with every movement. Even her reddish-blonde locks ditched their normal waves to stick to her face and neck. All in all, she felt ghastly as she waited at the front desk of the hotel, her thoughts consumed with nothing but clean, dry clothes. Intent on getting dried off as soon as possible, she didn't notice anything, or anyone, around her.

Suddenly, a familiar Escher design caught her eye. Black fish on a charcoal gray background mesmerized her. Suddenly all she could do was stand there, staring at those fish, not recognizing the design was on a man's tie.

The tie swayed; Maggie snapped back to reality noticing the tie was attached to a man with a pair of chocolate brown eyes.

A deep voice resonated from the smiling mouth below them, "I love Escher."

The timbre of his voice sent tiny sparks dancing along her spine, and she found herself blushing self-consciously. "Me too." Turning quickly toward the desk clerk, "Do I have any messages? Room 638?" she inquired.

The clerk glanced behind him, "No, ma'am."

"Thank you." Still flushed, Maggie managed a polite smile and then started toward the elevator.

Just before reaching the polished brass doors, she felt a large hand gently catch her sleeve, "Wait. I can't let another Escher lover walk away without us introducing ourselves."

Maggie's stomach jumped, and her mind went blank. Without explanation, she lunged for the open elevator, barely pulling her shopping bags through the doors before they shut.

Safe in her room, Maggie slammed her purse down on the bed. "Damn it!" She paced the room muttering, "All I had to do was answer him. I could've replied, 'My name is Maggie.' Or, 'Hello. Maggie O'Brien, and you are?' or, 'You have the most beautiful eyes, would you mind if I just stood here gazing into them?' Or something! But no, I took off and made an absolute ass of myself!"

Grabbing her phone, she speed-dialed her sister, forcing herself to inhale deeply while waiting through several rings.

The voice on the other end sounded cool and professional, "Good afternoon, Erickson Enterprises."

"Hey, Donna, it's Maggie. Is Kim available?"

"Hi, Maggie. How's New York? Has the conference started?"

The questions made Maggie smile. Of course, Donna would remember about this trip! "New York is rainy, but I had fun wandering around this afternoon. Tomorrow, I have to start earning my keep."

"Well, you needed some fun. Let me get Kim. She just finished reaming everyone out at the staff meeting, so she should be free and in a good mood."

A few moments later, Kim's voice rang cheerfully over the line. "Hey, Mags, what's up?"

"I made an ass of myself."

Maggie heard Kim swallow and couldn't repress a grin as she pictured the ever-present cup of coffee on her sister's desk.

"What'd you do now?"

Leave it to a sister to add the word 'now' to the question! Maggie grimaced. "I was waiting for messages at the hotel desk, and there was a guy wearing an Escher tie."

"You and your Escher infatuation. Go on."

"Well, I guess I was really staring at the tie. Then he moved and I realized I was staring. Before I had a chance to explain, he commented that he loves Escher too."

"Okay, makes sense. What's the problem?"

"The problem is, I turned eighty-three shades of red, mumbled a dumb 'me too,' and then tried to get the hell outta there! I mean, I was really staring, like a psycho or something." She sucked in a sharp breath. "But before I could get away, he stopped me and asked my name."

"Let me guess - you panicked and bolted?"

"Yeah! Not a word! Just *threw* myself into the elevator and didn't look back."

Kim paused, and Maggie heard her sip another jolt of caffeine. "What did he look like?"

"Huh?"

"The guy. What did he look like?" Kim prompted.

Reclining against the headboard, Maggie stared blindly at the ceiling. "Like, wow." A giggle bubbled up irresistibly. "Like a walking orgasm."

Kim laughed. "Go on!"

"He's really tall and muscular looking. Not like on steroids or anything, but like he could sweep you up in his arms effortlessly."

Her sister snorted, "Hey, Tinkerbell, *anyone* could sweep you up in his arms. You're a miniature freak of nature!"

All of her siblings had called her that for years, much to Maggie's chagrin. "Do you want me to tell you or not? He has really dark, almost black hair. Not long, but not short, with the tiniest bit of curl. And his eyes, they were amazing; the color of melted dark chocolate with lashes even longer than yours!"

"Wow. I guess he made an impression. What was he wearing?"

"I didn't really notice other than the tie."

"A wedding ring?"

"Kim! I'm telling you I stared, panicked, and ran like the wind. End of story! I wasn't checking out his ring finger. And now I feel really stupid because I could have at least given some sort of response other than bolting."

"Hello! You may not have looked at his finger, but you did look long enough to know he's gorgeous. Now, are you mad because you stared, because you ran, or because you didn't get his name?"

"Shit, I don't know. I mean the absolute last thing I need is a guy." Her voice quivered, "But some fun would be nice. Not that I'm really looking…but…you know."

"First of all, the thing you need most in life right now *is* a guy! Someone to remind you you're young and single. Someone who makes you feel like a woman, who makes you feel sexy and wanted. You're in New York without the boys! You should be having fun. I'm not suggesting you get married -- just have a fling. For God's sake, get laid!"

"Kim!"

"I mean it. Damn, Mags, you've built up this image of yourself as a nun or something."

"I'm a mother! I have to be a role model."

"The boys are here in Montreal, dipshit. You could be a pole dancer for the next couple of days and they'd never know. Do us all a favor and break out of your rut."

"Doesn't matter now, even if I did want to have some fun," Maggie moaned. "I ran away like an idiot, so even if he wanted to know my name, now he thinks I'm a total loser."

"Little sister, no man has ever looked at you and thought you were a loser. Most women would kill to look like you. Hell, you have the breasts of a goddess…"

"That's gross!"

"Oh, shut up, you know you do. You have Mom's build, which isn't fair at all. Then you have those friggin' great green eyes like Dad's."

Maggie giggled, "Okay, this is a really weird conversation but thank you."

Kim chuckled. "You're welcome, and you know I'd never blow smoke up your butt, so I'm telling you the truth. This thing today isn't a big deal. If you happen to run into him and he mentions it, lie like a rug, and tell him you had an upset stomach." She giggled conspiratorially. "Or just walk over and ask him to take you, right then and there. That would be *my* choice."

Maggie smiled. "Okay. I got it. I'll let you go."

"Love you. Call me if you see Mr. Wonderful again."

Chapter Four

The next morning, Maggie awoke in time to see the sunrise through the Manhattan skyline. For early April, the day was supposed to be unusually warm, and she looked forward to getting out in the spring weather.

She ambled into the bathroom to get dressed. No matter how much she was interested in the conference, she had to admit, the last thing she wanted to do was wear a bra and uncomfortable shoes while away from home. Slipping on a simple silk shift and low heels, she tried to ignore the lump in her throat, glancing at a photo of her boys on the bedside table before leaving. She admitted that although she missed them already, it felt nice to have a break, stay in a luxury hotel, and eat grown-up meals.

In the hotel dining room, Maggie searched for familiar faces from last year's conference. Seeing none, she resentfully ordered fruit and coffee. Although sausage and home fries sounded much more appealing, the idea of trotting an hour on the hotel treadmill made the fruit a much better choice. Opening her journal and beginning to write, she shut out the chattering around her.

So here I am in New York with my stupid journal full of blank pages.

Quickly erasing the word *stupid*, she eyed the journal thoughtfully.

I guess this is one of those times when I have to figure out whether or not to really put effort into something. I guess I need to do this (and do it well) if I want to be able to pay the bills next year. If all of this is confidential, I might as well tell it like it is.

I don't know what I want anymore. I love the boys more than anything in the world, but sometimes it would be nice to still be a woman — to be with someone, to have a life partner. Someone to talk, laugh, and cry with. God, the last time I had sex, I was married. And I really do love my job, but it isn't enough to keep me fantasy-free at night, when I'm finally alone for a few moments.

Yesterday I didn't get angry, but I made a stupid, rash decision. I was admiring a tie that a man in the lobby was wearing, and when he asked my name, I freaked and rushed off without answering. I was immediately embarrassed and angry with myself for not acknowledging him.

A deep voice brought her abruptly back to the present. "We meet again."

Maggie looked up. Way up. The man from the lobby stood there, dressed in a light gray blazer, but without the Escher tie.

"It seems we do," she responded warily.

"You ran away so quickly that I never caught your name." He held out a hand expectantly. "Actually, I asked, but you seem to have had an emergency before you could answer. I'm Andreas Serapes; friends call me Andre. I hope nothing was wrong yesterday."

Maggie shook his hand cautiously, feeling its warmth as it wrapped around hers. "See-rah-peas? That's an interesting name."

"It's Greek. My parents are originally from Athens. And you are?"

Maggie turned bright red again, feeling inept and awkward. "I'm Maggie." She cringed inwardly. "I apologize for running away, it was just an incidental emergency, really. I wasn't feeling well."

"Really?" He didn't bother to hide his disbelief.

Maggie blushed a deep rose. "No. Not really." She shifted uncomfortably. "I don't make a habit of staring, and I was a bit embarrassed to be caught. I do apologize for seeming rude."

"Apology accepted."

A smile spread across his face and Maggie noticed one perfect dimple in his right cheek. As he gestured toward the unoccupied chair, she made note of the way his shirt strained over his broad chest. "Do you feel apologetic enough to let me join you for breakfast?"

Her response was quick, "I would have to feel *pretty* guilty."

"True. Do you?" He raised a brow as Maggie sized him up, a smile tugging at her lips.

"I don't know. That's an awful lot of guilt. But I guess you can sit down." She hastily shoved her journal into her bag, tucking the bag under her chair. "Please join me."

Almost an hour later, Maggie pushed her coffee cup away. Looking at her watch, she pouted. "I have to run. Today is the first day of the conference, and I hate to be late for anything, regardless of what my boss may think." Standing, she brushed a crumb off the front of her dress.

Andre rose with her, his gaze dropping quickly, suggesting he was admiring her soft curves. "Thanks for keeping me company this morning. What a great way to start my day."

"You're welcome. It was my pleasure."

He eyed her in a way that made her suddenly feel warm, although the room itself was almost chilly. "Can I push your guilty conscience even further and convince you to have dinner with me tonight?"

The words rushed out of her mouth. "I'd love to have dinner with you." Suddenly she looked stricken. "Oh, shit. I forgot the reception this evening. I have to be there."

His eyes sparkled, "What time will you be done? Maybe still time for a drink?"

She thought about the schedule, "I should be done around nine-ish."

His smile made her nerves hum with a pleasant sense of anticipation. "I'll be in the lobby at nine. See you then."

Chapter Five

Somewhat before nine, Andre settled onto a sofa, providing him with a good view of the lobby. Picking up a newspaper, he scanned the headlines, trying not to look at his watch. When a small hand tapped his shoulder, he all but threw the paper aside, then stood, and smoothed the front of his blazer.

He smiled down at Maggie. The simple dress she wore earlier was replaced with a fitted, deep rose sheath stopping just above her knees, the hem a scalloped row of lace highlighting long slender legs below. Even with stiletto heels, he still towered above her. While her outfit was somewhat casual, it was alluring, and Andre realized with a start how much he was physically attracted to her.

"Hi. I was catching up on the news." She lifted an eyebrow in disbelief, and it was now his turn to look embarrassed. "No, not really. I was waiting for you but pretending to seem aloof."

He shrugged. "Now that I admitted that I'll add that you look great, and I'm really glad you're here." His eyes caressed her warmly. "I spent the day wishing it was already nine o'clock."

Maggie batted her lashes; glad she spent so much time on her appearance. "Me too." She gestured toward the front door of the lobby. "Let's get out of here."

Despite the hour, the streets were crowded, and Maggie let Andre lead, admiring the easy way he moved. Several times, when they arrived at especially crowded areas, he would step slightly to the side as he gently placed his hand on her lower back, guiding her in front of him, making her feel protected and special. Finally, he motioned toward a row of outdoor cafes. "Would you mind going to one of these? Or would you prefer to sit inside?"

Maggie restrained the urge to tell him anywhere was fine as long as he was there. Clearing her throat, she answered, "Outside sounds great. I've been stuck in windowless rooms all day, and it's still nice and warm out."

"This one has a back patio. That should be quieter."

Entering the nearest café, they sat at a secluded corner table. A small white candle flickered in the center, throwing shadows on their faces. Andre smiled at her, "Wine, beer, something else?"

"Wine would be great."

"Red or white?"

Maggie smiled, "Red. White is just for making spritzers once a year."

"Ah, a woman after my own heart!" Andre ordered a bottle of Cabernet, and they watched the other customers milling about as they waited.

Once the wine was poured and then tasted, Andre leaned back in his chair and allowed his eyes to soak in Maggie's face. Her green eyes glowed in the candlelight.

She began to feel uncomfortable under his scrutiny. Then he smiled at her, and she recognized the admiration in his eyes. Its warmth slowly spread through her, like the heady wine.

Never taking his eyes off her, he rolled a sip of wine over his tongue before speaking. "Okay, Maggie. So far, I know almost nothing about you. We talked weather and national news this morning, not much more. I know you're in Manhattan for some sort of a conference, you drink your coffee with cream but no sugar, and you like Escher."

The wine threw off ruby sparks as Maggie twirled her glass lightly between her fingers. She hesitated for a moment, trying in vain to think of a clever and flirtatious answer. "What do you want to know?"

"Everything. Anything."

The words should have sounded desperate, but his voice was so sincere that Maggie found it unbearably seductive.

"Maybe I should say I want to know everything about you, but I'll settle for anything you feel comfortable telling me." He leaned forward. "I plan to know you very well," he whispered conspiratorially.

Maggie's eyes widened. "I have absolutely no idea what to say now."

"Start with the simple things. What do you do? Why? Why are you in Manhattan this week?"

Maggie debated briefly how much to share with him, feeling both the pull to tell him all, and the need to make sure she wasn't making herself vulnerable. In the few seconds it took to feel both of those emotions, she realized old emotional scars still lingered close to the surface and reminded herself to keep her answers fairly neutral. For a moment, she wondered if she would ever feel fully safe again, then shook off the thought. Andre had asked simple questions; ones she could answer. "I'm here for a national conference on program options in Special Education."

"Would you be offended if I asked you to explain that in English?"

Maggie laughed and sipped her wine. Brushing a wayward curl back from her temple, she grinned. "Special Education is the simple name for the part of the public education system that provides a 'free and appropriate education' for all students regardless of their abilities or problems."

He nodded slowly. "That part I understand. I took several educational law classes at Georgetown."

"This conference is looking at changes in the law covering Special Education."

He tipped his head, his interest piqued. "So, are you a lawyer or an educator?"

"I'm an educational psychologist."

"What exactly is an *educational psychologist*?"

"It means I'm both a clinical psychologist and an educator."

"So, what do you do on a normal workday?"

"There is no such thing." She grinned again. "I'm the director of an educational program where we train new teachers through a high school program for students with social, emotional, and mental health disabilities. I monitor the student teachers; do some of the therapeutic work, and one semester a year, I teach one course of abnormal psychology to undergraduates."

"So, you have your doctorate?"

She looked uncomfortable, knowing how people usually responded when she answered that question. "I actually have two doctorates. One is in clinical psychology; one is in educational leadership."

"Wow," he said, and sipped his wine, "Knowing how hard my sister worked for her doctorate, I can't imagine going for two of them."

She shrugged, "I get bored easily. Just one didn't cover everything I wanted to know." Maggie slowly inhaled and sat up straight. Swallowing, she waved a hand. "That's what I do. Now, it's your turn in the hot seat. What do you do and why are you here?"

Leaning forward, Andre lifted her glass to refill it. Handing it back, his fingers brushed hers. When she didn't resist, Andre stroked them and smiled as he noticed her eyes darken. "What was the question?"

"Everything. Anything." Maggie's gaze didn't waver. Her eyes sparkled mischievously as she wet her lower lip with the tip of her tongue. "You know, start with the simple things."

Andre's body responded instantly to the glimpse of her tongue as he imagined tasting her lips with his own. "I live in Boston and I'm the head of a small law firm.

Most of the time we represent criminal, employment, and business law; I'm here for the National Bar Association conference."

"Isn't the combination of fields unusual? I thought lawyers usually picked criminal, family, or business."

He shrugged, "I started as a prosecutor, liked the criminal stuff, but then got to a point where some of it felt morally wrong. I took on partners, so we diversified. Most of the time, I work the employment cases."

They continued to talk quietly as the night wore on. The bottle of wine had been empty for some time when Andre looked at his watch with surprise. "I apologize, Maggie. We should go."

Startled, Maggie didn't understand why he was apologizing. Had she done something wrong? After all, she hadn't dated a relative stranger in many years. Maybe the rules had changed. Even in the shadowy garden, Andre saw her cheeks turn dark red.

"Oh, okay." Gathering her purse, she stood. "Thank you for tonight."

Andre stood up quickly, instantly understanding her thoughts. His hands were firm as he put them on her upper arms. "Maggie! I was apologizing because I was so involved in our conversation, I didn't realize how late it is, and you've had a long day. I felt badly that I didn't consider you might be tired." His hands slid down her arms until he was holding both of her hands, "I had a wonderful time with you." Stepping closer, he lowered his voice, "I had a *more* than wonderful time." With one finger, he tipped her chin up, his tone commanding, "Maggie, look at me."

Slowly tilting her head and looking him in the eye, her eyes were clear evidence she didn't believe him. "Maggie. Listen to me. If I didn't think it was too soon, and that you'd understandably slap me for trying, I'd ask you to come back to my room with me. I had a wonderful time with you tonight, and I hope you'll believe me enough to have breakfast with me tomorrow, and dinner tomorrow night, for that matter."

"Really?" Maggie chewed hard on her lower lip.

"Really." He leaned close enough for her to feel the heat of his body. "I really mean it. And stop chewing on that gorgeous lip."

Before Maggie knew what was happening, his mouth descended on hers. The world tipped dangerously, and Maggie moved closer to the only thing that seemed stable. Andre's arms wrapped around her, and she savored the warmth of his hard chest pressed against her.

Moments later, Andre regretfully pulled back. "I'm sorry again, Maggie." He put up a silencing finger, "Wait! Before you get defensive again, listen to me. I'm not sorry I kissed you, but that I did it here. I admit I spent a lot of time today thinking about what it would be like to kiss you, but I pictured a much more romantic spot, preferably without an audience."

Maggie had never kissed a virtual stranger before. She glowed with reckless excitement. "Don't be sorry. I don't mind that our first kiss was here. Not at all."

His chuckle sounded deep and sexy. "Oh, you don't, do you? Then maybe I should kiss you again."

"Maybe you should."

In the elevator, Andre kept a warm arm around Maggie. "Breakfast tomorrow?"

She shook her head unhappily, "The first session tomorrow is a breakfast meeting, and I really need to be there."

"Then something later?"

"Definitely."

At her floor, they stepped off the elevator and walked toward her room. Maggie leaned up against her door, "Thank you for tonight."

"My pleasure." His smile was slow and sexy, "Good night, Maggie." He leaned down to kiss her, his hands caressing her shoulders, "Sleep well."

"Good night."

Back in her hotel room, Maggie sat in the armchair looking out at the city, her journal on her lap. She wrote:

*So tonight, I did something completely unlike me. I went out for drinks with the Escher guy, Andre. He came over and introduced himself at breakfast, and then later asked me to dinner, which I couldn't do, but we went out for drinks tonight. I don't think I've ever gone out on a date with someone that soon after meeting them. Then, at the end of the evening, he kissed me. I know **that's** never happened that fast before. So, the question is, did I move this fast because I'm trying to prove something, or because something about this guy got under my skin this fast? I mean, no matter what, this can only be a fling. I'm only here for a couple more days. He's from Boston, so it's not like we can start long distance dating, I mean, what the heck would I do with the boys? I don't even know if he likes kids, or frankly, if he has any of his own.*

The one thing I did notice when we were out tonight, is that I still am pretty wary of letting anyone know much of anything about me. I can dodge personal questions like a pro, but damn, it would be nice to feel safe enough in the world that I don't feel like I need to keep up the smokescreen.

So, I guess I need to figure out, if I hear from him again — which I sure hope I do — how far I'm willing to take this.

Chapter Six

The next afternoon, Maggie walked back to the hotel with a group from the conference. Trying to keep up with the conversation, her thoughts irresistibly returned to the magical night before. Despite the heat, she shivered happily when she remembered the feel of Andre's arm around her as they walked back to the hotel.

In the elevator, Maggie pushed the sweat-damp hair from her forehead. Her dress stuck to the small of her back, and her thighs chafed in the heat. She longed for a cool shower and fresh clothes as she dragged herself off the elevator.

Startled to see a long white box leaning against the door to her room, she juggled her purse and notebook, reaching for it tentatively.

Once inside her room, she placed the box reverently on the bed. The gold ribbon slid off neatly despite her shaking fingers. Nestled amongst white tissue paper was one perfect, dark red, long-stemmed rose. Tucked in its leaves was an ivory card.

Forgetting her earlier desire for a shower, Maggie sat down. Holding the rose carefully, she breathed in its heady scent. Almost purring, she slid her fingernail under the flap of the envelope. The note was brief:

I missed you today. Call me when you get back, Room 1118, Andre

Instinctively, Maggie reached for the phone to call her sister. As soon as Kim came on the line, Maggie gushed, "He sent me a rose, just because!"

Kim's confusion was clear in her voice. "Who?"

"The Escher guy! His name is Andre."

"Oh, my god! Did you sleep with him?"

Maggie almost shouted, "No, I didn't sleep with him!"

"Why not?"

"Kim! Listen!"

The tone was emphatic. "I *am* listening."

"We had drinks last night at a café. He's a lawyer, he's gorgeous, and drop-dead sexy, and..." Her voice trailed off happily. "I just found it when I came back to my room. It's sitting here beside me. A perfect, long-stemmed, dark red rose. With a note saying he missed me today."

"No way! A lawyer? Damn, how do you manage these things? Even Mom couldn't complain about a lawyer."

"Honest to God! And, I mean, he had no reason to send a rose. We just had drinks, and then he kissed me, and we're having dinner tonight, and he's so wonderful." Maggie gushed.

"Back the info-train up! What the hell do you mean, he kissed you? Spill!" her sister insisted.

"Oh, Kim. He kisses like a god. I mean, I got hot just from kissing, no hands anywhere, and I was ready. Can you imagine?"

Kim's voice suggested a hint of envy. "That's so awesome, Mags. But what are you doing talking to me? Go call him!" she instructed.

Nervous and excited, Maggie sat back against the pillows and took a deep breath. Picking up the rose, she cradled its velvety petals, unconsciously resting it between the gentle swells of her breasts. Taking in its enticing scent, she dialed carefully.

"Hello?" His rich voice instantly raised goosebumps on her arms.

"Hi. It's me." Maggie couldn't suppress a huge grin.

In his suite, Andre also smiled. He pictured her sitting in her room and couldn't help but wonder what she was wearing. An irresistible image of Maggie wearing nothing but the rose, was painfully arousing. He shifted uncomfortably. "Me? Who's 'me?'"

"The recipient of that beautiful rose."

"Which recipient? I sent several roses today."

Her squeak was unintentional. "You what?"

The deep rumble of Andre's laugh made her clutch the rose to her breasts. When a thorn pricked at her delicate skin, she sniffed in surprise.

"Just kidding." His voice softened, "Only to you. You're the only person I missed today."

"I missed you too."

"I was beginning to think you weren't ever coming back."

She chuckled, "I gather patience isn't one of your virtues?"

"Not where you are concerned."

His answer increased her heart rate. "The last session went long, and I was sitting up front so I couldn't escape without everyone seeing me. Then I was walking back with some colleagues, and the streets were mobbed, so it took us a while. How was your day?"

"Pretty decent. We cut the afternoon session short because the air conditioning wasn't working. Lawyers don't do discomfort." His voice was wry. "So, I actually had part of the afternoon free. I tried calling you earlier, just hoping you'd be around. We could've played hooky together."

Maggie's mind filled with things they could have done during a free afternoon, and heat flooded her. "That would've been great." She shifted on her bed, and her voice became more formal. "Thank you for the rose, it's perfect." Then her voice softened again. "I'm just sitting here stroking the petals. I can't seem to let go of it."

Andre gripped the receiver harder, struggling vainly to reverse the way his body came to attention. He cleared his throat. "You're welcome, it was my pleasure. Are we still on for tonight, or are you too worn out from your class?"

"I'd love to do something. What do you have in mind?"

"Why not dinner and a movie? We can make sure both places are air conditioned."

Maggie's voice radiated happiness. "Oh, that sounds great! I haven't been to a movie theater in forever. Why don't I come up as soon as I'm ready? I have to make a few calls, and then I desperately need a shower."

"Perfect. Hurry."

Refreshed by the shower, Maggie found herself hesitating in front of her closet. Tucked to one side of her undeniably sedate wardrobe was a small black dress her sister sent from Montreal. Maggie threw it in her suitcase at the last moment, hoping maybe there might be an occasion to wear it. The dress tied around the neck, leaving much of her back bare, while the skirt stopped quite a bit above her knees; it was definitely not her normal look. Kim even included tiny, black silk panties to wear underneath. Feeling like the wild woman she'd never been, Maggie reached for the dress.

Checking herself in the mirror, she was thrilled. Kim was right; the dress worked. Her heart beat faster as she imagined Andre discovering the wisp of silk under it.

At Andre's door, she took a steadying breath and knocked softly. He appeared quickly. "Hi."

He drew her inside and let the door swing shut as his finger traced a line down her bare arm. His eyes swept over every inch of her, and Maggie felt his gaze as intently as if he was touching her, everywhere. "You're stunning." Leaning down, he kissed her lingeringly. "You do know this little dress of yours will drive me insane."

Maggie's body felt weak at his touch, "I decided to go with a slightly different look tonight. I'm glad you like it."

He smiled appreciatively, "It should be your everyday look."

Trying to calm herself, she stretched up and kissed his cheek, tantalized by his clean masculine smell. "Thank you again for the rose. It was a wonderful surprise!"

He tugged on a piece of hair curling at the nape of her neck. "That's it? You call that a thank you kiss?"

"Yes, I do. Do you have a different idea?"

His grin was devilish but seemed to promise heaven. "Let's see." At first, the touch of his mouth was delicate, but then he pulled her close. His hands were firm on her back, his mouth hungrily devouring hers. As his tongue slipped into her mouth, Maggie was momentarily startled before she cooed happily. Her arms tightening around him, her senses swam, and her fingers soon weaved through his dark hair. His long fingers dipped into the back of her dress as he growled appreciatively, finding only bare skin.

Long minutes later, they pulled apart, breathless and flushed. "*That's* a thank you kiss."

Straightening her dress, Maggie tried to control the tremble in her voice. "I'll try to remember that."

Andre tucked a curl behind her ear, his fingers lingering on her cheek. "Damn, Maggie." He took a deep breath. "I just want you to know I don't usually move this fast but can't seem to help myself where you're concerned. Tell me if I'm pushing you too fast. Would you…" He nearly growled when his cell phone chirped shrilly on the end table. "I can't believe it. *Now*? The phone rings *right now*?"

Maggie kissed his cheek. "I'm not going anywhere. Answer the phone and we can finish our conversation later."

Chapter Seven

Maggie stood looking out the window. She jumped as Andre's finger found its way down her bare spine. Still on the phone, he handed her a hastily scrawled note.

Feel free to look around; this should only take a minute.

While Andre continued what was obviously a business conversation, Maggie wandered around his suite looking through the open doorways. Her own room was nice, but paled in comparison to this. Andre's included a master bedroom with a king-sized bed and Jacuzzi tub in the bathroom, a sitting room and a dining/kitchen area he was obviously using as an office. An impossibly thin laptop sat open on the dining table next to a compact portable fax machine. Neat files were spread around the computer, and Mozart played softly on a nearby stereo.

Everything in the room spoke of a successful urban professional, and for a moment, Maggie felt uncertain. She hardly considered herself the type of woman who belonged with a sophisticated businessman like this; this seemed more like a "Kim-sort-of-situation," somehow.

A small frown creased her brow as she whispered, "What the hell am I doing here?"

She was so immersed in her thoughts that she didn't hear Andre behind her. Still on the phone, he leaned down to quickly kiss the back of her neck. She gasped and moved away, startled, and embarrassed by the tightening of her nipples through the thin fabric of the dress.

Andre's eyes darkened as he realized how sensitive Maggie was to his touch. His own body responded instantly. Still watching her, he picked up the newly printed pages on the fax tray. "Okay, Dennis. The fax is here. I'll take a look at it. You can't file this tonight, anyway. I'll review it first thing tomorrow and fax back any changes before office hours tomorrow." His voice was soothing. "Stop worrying, it sounds like you handled the situation beautifully. Good night."

Ending the call, he turned toward Maggie. "I'm sorry that took so long. Problems at the office."

Brushing her fingers over the edge of the table, Maggie tried to think. "Andre, can I ask a question?"

He pulled her close. "Anything."

"If I weren't here, I mean, if you didn't have plans with me, would you deal with the fax right now?"

He shrugged. "Probably. But I have plans for you and that little black dress tonight, and legal motions aren't part of them."

Maggie took his hands off her waist. "Look them over now and *then* we can get dinner."

"Maggie!" He frowned impatiently. "We're going out to dinner; the motion can wait."

Her voice was certain, "I'd really feel better if you did that first. I mean, it sounds like whoever Dennis is, he's stressed. It seems wrong to be having fun while he's getting heartburn." She shrugged, "I can either wait here, or go back to my room and you can come get me when you're done. Please, Andre." She implored.

He growled, "I don't think I've ever had a woman say she preferred me working than taking her out." He leaned down to kiss her nose. "But then again, I've never met anyone like you."

"So, you'll do it?"

"As long as you stay right here."

Maggie watched TV while Andre worked. When he began reading parts of the motion aloud, she struggled to hide a smile.

He raised an eyebrow. "I'm glad you find this amusing. This is your fault, remember? You're the one who insisted."

Maggie walked over to rub his shoulders. "It's just funny to hear a lawyer talking to himself. Somehow, I imagined that legal gobbledygook would just gush forth automatically."

With a lightning move, Andre swept Maggie onto his lap. "Are you spending a lot of time imagining lawyers?" His fingers stroked her ribcage and made her gasp. "Are you?"

She ran her fingers lightly over his cheeks, loving the slightly rough, masculine feel of his skin. "Only you."

"Good," he growled. As he kissed her, his hands roamed her bare back, pulling her closer, enjoying the feel of her wrapped in his arms.

Maggie pulled back, breathing hard. "Finish the damn motion." She ran a finger over his mouth. "Finish it, so we can get on with the evening."

A few minutes later, Andre looked up to see Maggie curled up on the couch, her bare legs tucked under her. "I swear, I'm almost done. Would you like to order something to eat or drink from room service to tide you over?"

Maggie realized she needed to make a decision. They could still go out to dinner. Or she could suggest ordering in, knowing where that might lead.

Andre's expression turned quizzical. "Maggie. Did you hear me?"

Maggie's face was almost painfully serious. Unconsciously, she began to rub the hem of her dress. Then, as though something released inside her, she nodded. Her voice was soft, but sure. "Andre, you shouldn't rush what you're doing. Why don't we order dinner in?"

His eyes widened, unsure of her intention. "So, you want to stay here?" He paused. "For dinner?"

"For dinner." Just how does a woman ask a man if she can spend the night? Maggie forced herself to speak casually. "And, you know, after dinner we could watch a movie here or something…"

Her cheeks were so red that Andre only imagined how hard it was for her to say that. "Maggie, you know

I'd love you to stay. To watch a movie." He grinned. "Or—*something*."

Maggie released a breath she didn't know she was holding and laughed nervously. Walking over to the couch, he pulled her to her feet, holding her close. "Now. First of all, let me tell you, the idea of you staying for dinner, or something, will make concentrating on that damn motion almost impossible."

Her head resting on his broad chest, Maggie felt the heat of his skin and the deep rumble of his voice.

"But I really am almost done. Why don't you think about what you want for dinner, and we can order in a few minutes?"

An hour later, Maggie carried the empty Chinese containers to the garbage can in the kitchenette. With an embarrassed grin, she looked at Andre. "This sounds really stupid, but I need to brush my teeth."

"Well, I can offer two options. You can borrow my toothbrush. Or I can call down to the desk for one."

Maggie spoke without thinking. "Or I can take a run downstairs and use my own."

"You could do that." Andre debated for a moment then took her hands. "I have to say this." He touched her face tenderly. "I have absolutely no idea where we're headed here. I don't usually try to lure women to my hotel room when I barely know them. I mean," he grinned wickedly, "I certainly hope I know where we're headed over the next few hours, but if you want to run downstairs to brush your teeth, do. And if you come back up, and you want to just watch a movie, that's okay too."

Maggie started to speak, but he interrupted her. "Wait. What I'm trying to say is, I want this to feel right to you." Then he looked embarrassed. "I'm sorry I interrupted you."

She smiled. "It's okay. I was just going to say that if you really don't mind me borrowing your toothbrush, that would be great."

"Oh." His chuckle made her smile. "Wow. I really overdid it, didn't I?"

"No." She stretched so that her body barely touched his. "You were being kind. Thank you. But I suggested staying in for dinner because I wanted to stay here." As he drew in a breath to speak, she kissed him quickly. "With you; with no interruptions, spectators, or anything to distract us." Her grin was mischievous. "But you have to turn off all of your machines."

Andre couldn't stop kissing her. Her arms encircled his neck and her breasts pressed against the thin fabric of his shirt. He stooped slightly to slide his arm under her knees, sweeping her into his arms.

Long moments later, Maggie broke the kiss, completely breathless. His passion was almost dizzying, and she needed a moment to acclimate. "How about a glass of wine on the couch?"

Chapter Eight

After room service delivered the wine, in less than five minutes Maggie and Andre sat entwined on the couch, sipping slowly, watching a British comedy on television. When the bottle was empty, Maggie stood, teetering as she carried it to the kitchen. Andre followed her, kissing her neck as she rinsed the glasses. "Leave those, the maid will get them in the morning."

"It will only take a second."

He lightly nipped her earlobe.

Maggie giggled. "Stop it." He stopped and she whimpered, "I didn't really mean it."

"Oh, you didn't?" He raised an eyebrow. "Then I won't stop until you leave," he stroked her bare arm slowly, seeing her body respond instantly, "hopefully tomorrow morning."

"Definitely tomorrow morning." A tiny shiver of nervousness rippled through her. She felt as though she just jumped out of an airplane, praying her parachute opened before she hit the ground.

Andre bent down to kiss her deeply before sweeping her into his arms and moving toward his bedroom.

The room was dark except for the light of a small lamp in the corner. Andre placed Maggie reverently on the bed, before moving to sit beside her. "Are you sure?"

Maggie moved so she knelt next to him, and kissed his cheek, then stood facing him. "More than sure." Slowly she unbuttoned his shirt, before tugging it from the waistband of his pants. Sliding it from his shoulders, she gave a small smile, entranced. His broad shoulders tapered to a narrow waist with dark hair sprinkled lightly over his muscular chest. Using just her fingertips, Maggie lightly touched his skin, delighting in the feel of it and the way his body responded.

Andre watched Maggie, sensing her need to be in control, willing to allow her that for the moment. As her fingers reached the waistband of his pants, he stood.

She protested. "I'm not done."

His voice caressed her. "I didn't say you were; I thought I'd make it easier for you."

"How considerate." Slowly, she slid his pants down his well muscled thighs. Seeing his manhood press against the thin fabric of his silk boxers, Maggie felt lightheaded with primal instinct. Heat flooded her, as desire radiated between them. She tossed his pants blindly aside and lightly caressed him.

Andre couldn't stand any more. He insisted, "My turn!"

"But…" Maggie's reply was lost as Andre untied her dress with one deft movement, letting the fabric glide down to the floor. His hands cupped her breasts as he pressed her onto the bed and into the pillows. His thumbs brushed her nipples, causing her to arch her back, wanting more.

He laid her down on the cool comforter, and she was barely conscious of his body shifting until the soft touch of his hands was replaced by his insistent tongue. All coherent thoughts left her.

Maggie wanted to feel him too. Without hesitation, she moved both hands to cup him, reveling in his instant response. Impatiently, she pushed aside the last of his clothing to release his heavy length.

Her dress sliding away, Maggie felt vulnerable. Only the tiniest scrap of silk remained between them.

Looking into Andre's eyes, her craving instantly replaced any doubts.

"God, Maggie. You're so beautiful." He ran his tongue down the hollow between her breasts. "So incredibly sexy." His tongue continued down her smooth stomach until he reached the black triangle of silk. "And part of what makes you so very sexy is that you don't know it. You have no idea what looking at you does to me. Or touching you." His breath was warm through the silk. "Or tasting you."

Pushing the silk aside, his tongue delved into her warmth. Maggie's soft cry of pleasure was all the invitation he needed to continue his exploration.

Maggie felt crazed with her need for him. Waves of ecstasy washed over her until she could take no more. "Andre, please," she begged.

With one more lingering lick, he stopped. "Please, what?"

"Please. Now. I want you inside me."

With fluid grace, Andre moved above her. Maggie's hands clutched at his back as she urged him inside her, shuddering.

The next morning, Maggie awoke in an unfamiliar bed, wrapped in Andre's arms. A panic spread through her as she realized what she'd done.

Carefully, she slipped from the bed and into the bathroom. In the harsh fluorescent light, her eyes looked bloodshot and tired as they filled with tears. *Shit. I look like hell. I should know better than to sleep with makeup on, especially when I'm apt to wake up with a hangover. What the hell was I thinking? I slept with a guy I know nothing about. He doesn't even know I have kids, I never got his medical information, and no one knows where I am. What the hell makes me think this could work? I chase my neighbor's cows when they get loose and he's like a cultured demigod. What have I done?* Tears spilled down her cheeks as she tried to calm her breathing.

Wiping her face, she slipped back into the bedroom, looking for her clothes. Turning, she realized Andre was watching her. Feeling rumpled and unattractive, he looked perfect, his broad chest golden against the pure white of the sheets. "Come back to bed. It's too early to be up yet." He smiled enticingly. "I'll miss you beside me."

Maggie's heart ached. "I have to get to my first session. And I need a shower and clothes first."

"Maggie. It's only six o'clock. Come back to bed for a bit and then we'll get some breakfast." He held out his hand. "Come on over here and tell me why you look anxious."

Slowly, Maggie walked over to the side of the bed. He tugged her hand, pulling her down so she was sitting next to him, and rubbed her back. "Talk to me."

Maggie blushed. "I've never done this before."

"Done what?" He sounded confused.

"You know, stayed overnight with someone I don't really know. And I don't know where this is going."

Andre bunched pillows behind his head to look at her more comfortably. "Maggie, I don't, as you put it, stay overnight with strangers either." He ran one finger slowly down the side of her neck, noting her shiver with anticipation. "Or, as I would put it, I don't make passionate love with a woman if I don't plan to be there in the morning. Or the next night, or the next week."

"What are you saying?" Maggie pressed.

He sat forward to kiss her lightly. "I'm saying I went into last night trying to figure out how we can make this work, us being apart, when I have spent the last two days absolutely filled with thoughts of you. I don't have one-night stands with anyone. And for me, this certainly wasn't one." He tipped her chin, peering into her eyes, "Was it for you?"

She rubbed her temple, "No. I mean, I don't know. I came to New York looking to break out of my rut, as my sister calls it, and I guess I was more willing than usual to be open to new experiences. But, no, I don't have flings either."

"Okay then. I'm going to tuck you back into bed with me for a while, then we'll have breakfast and figure out how to make this work." He pulled her to lie down beside him, "Maggie, I've never fallen for someone like this before. C'mon, come back to bed for a bit."

It wasn't just a one-nighter! With an anticipation-filled giggle, Maggie slipped back under the duvet.

An hour later, Maggie stretched happily. "Okay, now I really have to change and get ready."

"Breakfast in an hour?"

"Perfect."

Pulling one of his t-shirts over her dress, she turned to look at him. "It's probably too late to ask this, but you're not married, are you? I mean, I'm not, so I'm hoping you're not," she ventured.

"Bit late to think of that, don't you think?" He rubbed his chin. "Happily divorced, thank you."

His response confused her. "Why happily?"

"Oh, it was pretty ugly. I count myself as lucky to have escaped."

"Really?"

"Yeah, the marriage was probably doomed right from the beginning; we were lucky to figure that out before we had any children."

"Didn't you want children?"

He shook his head, perfectly relaxed. "No. I know that doesn't sound politically correct in a time of larger suburban families and minivans, but I don't want kids."

Maggie felt her stomach lurch and tried to control her facial muscles.

"I don't feel comfortable around them. I'm not a patient person, so I tend to get frustrated and irritated by them. I love my life the way it is, with the freedom to do as I please without anyone needing my care or taking up my free time." His smile was sexy as he looked her up and down. "So, I can devote myself to you, for instance. Without kids to control my schedule, I can suggest we meet somewhere next weekend."

"That sounds perfect." Maggie tried to keep her voice steady as her stomach churned. "Okay, I have to run if I want a shower before breakfast."

Andre stood, completely comfortable in his nakedness. His kiss was sure and alluring. "See you in an hour."

Chapter Nine

Sitting in the airport, Maggie called her sister.

"This better be good, I'm still sleeping."

"Help." Maggie's voice dripped sadness.

Kim immediately sounded wide awake. "Oh, my God! You did it! And now you're freaking."

"How can you tell?"

"Because I know everything. What the hell happened?"

Maggie remembered every detail in a flash. "We ordered dinner in, and then, well, one thing led to another." Her voice trailed.

"You mean one thing led to getting naked?"

"Yeah. That's what I mean. Anyway. We did it once. Then we drank champagne, and then took a bath in his

Jacuzzi. Then he asked me to stay the night. We got up this morning and…"

"Damn! When you decide to loosen up, you go all the way! How was it? Did the earth move? Did angels weep?" she teased.

"Both. Repeatedly." Then Maggie's voice broke, "And he's divorced and doesn't want children. The way he said it, it's not that he didn't want children with his ex-wife; it's that he doesn't want children *at all*."

Kim understood instantly. "Oh, shit. What are you going to do?"

"I'm at the airport and I'm going home to hide."

"Maggie! You can't just run away from him like that."

"I didn't tell him about the boys, and now it's too late. I have to just get out of here, that's it."

"What if he tries to contact you?"

Maggie shook her head, "I don't think he can find me. I used O'Brien as my last name for the conference, everything at the college and all my public records are a mix of Erickson and Magdalena too, so if he's so inclined to search, he'll be looking for Maggie O'Brien."

Kim paused on the other end. "Okay. I still think you should have told him the truth, but I get it."

Maggie's voice broke. "It wouldn't matter anyway, Kim. He's like fine champagne, and I'm like Budweiser."

Chapter Ten

Striding into the lobby, Andre felt on top of the world. He couldn't wait to see Maggie. Maybe he could convince her to stay in New York for another few nights with him without the distractions of the conferences. He smiled thinking of the night before, and how amazing it was to meet her when he wasn't looking to meet anyone.

He searched the couches for her in vain. Realizing she wasn't there, he looked into the restaurant and didn't see her there either. Increasingly concerned, he approached the front desk and waited impatiently for the clerk.

"Yes. May I help you, sir?"

Andre turned his head again, checking the lobby one more time. "I was wondering if you've seen Maggie

O'Brien this morning. Room 638?" Andre didn't stop to think that maybe the desk clerk might not know who she was.

Shaking his head, the clerk answered, "No, sir. I haven't seen her, but I just came on duty. Would you like me to call her room?"

"Please."

As the clerk dialed, he shuffled through a pile of papers. He abruptly put down the phone. "Mr. Serapes, sir, Ms. O'Brien checked out this morning."

"What?" Andre's mind went blank. "She checked out?"

"Yes, sir. Just about forty-five minutes ago."

"Are you sure?"

"It's right here," the clerk said, motioning toward his paperwork.

"But we had plans for today!"

"I'm sorry, Mr. Serapes. I wish I could be more helpful."

An older man stepped up beside the clerk. "Mr. Serapes, I handled Ms. O'Brien's check-out. She mentioned something urgent came up, but she did leave a note." He handed Andre a small ivory envelope.

Sitting down heavily on a nearby chair, Andre's finger quickly unsealed the flap, only to find a brief note.

Andre — Something has come up, and I need to head home right away. I apologize for leaving without saying a proper goodbye. Thank you for some incredible memories. All the best, Maggie

Andre read and reread the note, searching for a clue as to why she left, but found none. His stomach clenched, and he felt dizzy. Hurrying to the front desk, his tone was desperate. "Do you have an address or phone number for her?"

The clerk looked uncomfortable. "I'm sorry, sir. All guest records are confidential."

Andre's face mottled with rage as he leaned over the counter. "I need to find her! All I need is an address, phone number, email, anything!"

From the back office, the manager raced out, "Mr. Serapes! Please calm down. We can't give you any information."

Andre needed them to understand how much he needed a way to contact her. "Just a phone number!" he pleaded.

"I'm sorry."

Ten minutes later, Andre sat at the table in his room, Googling Maggie's name, trying to find any way to contact her. An hour later, admitting defeat, he picked up the phone to call the private investigator used by his firm. "Dan, I need you to find someone for me."

The investigator in his office in Boston paused on the other line. "Andre, you never called me direct before. This must be important."

"It is, Dan. Can you help me?"

"Sure," Dan said, after another pause. "Who am I looking for?"

"Maggie O'Brien. She's a college professor. Unfortunately, that's all I got."

Chapter Eleven

Maggie's stomach rolled as the plane descended into Burlington. Her nerves hummed with sadness, and she couldn't wait to get home and let the impending tears fall.

An hour and a half later, she pulled into her driveway. Lugging her bags inside, she dumped them in the doorway of the laundry room, immediately hitting the play button on the answering machine.

Beep – "Hi, Mags, it's Mike. I deposited the rent checks; the deposit slip is on the fridge. I watered the plants and stuck a chlorine stick in the pool. Call me when you get back, I'll buy you dinner."

Beep – "Maggie, this is Sheila from Dr. Robinson's office. Just wanted to remind you about your appointment Monday night."

As if I could forget that shit, she thought.

Beep – "Maggie, it's Kim. Mom and Dad took the boys to the Biodome, so I'm home sitting next to the phone. Call me."

Maggie sat down on the stool next to the phone and hit the speed dial. "Hey, it's me."

"How was your flight?"

"Okay. I guess." Her voice broke. "Damn, Kim, I really liked this guy."

Kim's voice was soothing. "I know, sweetie. Maybe it'll still work out."

"No, it won't. He doesn't seem the type to change his mind over something as big as not wanting children. I expect he's pretty pissed off right now since I just bolted with no explanation."

"Give it time. Maybe it will work out, and if it doesn't, at least you tried living again."

"So why do I feel like I just died?"

Chapter Twelve

Two nights later, Maggie sat on her back deck after the boys went to sleep, her journal next to her on the arm of the chair.

I haven't written anything in the last few days. My last entry was about the incredible evening I had with Andre in New York. After that, we spent more and more time together. Then he told me he didn't have any children, and really doesn't want children, and doesn't even like them. In reflecting on the whole thing, I should have told him about the boys from the very beginning. I was trying too hard to have fun myself. In the future, I need to remember that no matter what, I am a mom first.

Over the next several weeks, Maggie wrote in her journal more often:

I'm bored, not that I have any free time, but I want to have more of my own life. Not saying the boys don't come first, but by the time I've taken care of them, my big thrill is watching a little bit of TV before bed. I need to find a hobby or something to release my pent-up adult energy.

Then,

So tonight, at dinner, Nick asked if I was ever going to have a boyfriend. Then Eli got into the conversation saying that his friends all have a mom and dad who live together. We had a long conversation about how much both Daddy and I love them, and that not all mommies and daddies are together or have a partner.

Almost two months after New York, Maggie sat on the couch, and wrote:

*The good thing about being so busy with swimming lessons, the garden, soccer, and all the other kid stuff in the summer is that I don't have a lot of time to think, and by the end of the day, I'm so tired I just collapse. But if I was looking at myself clinically, I'd say that I need to get my own shit together. I am so kid-focused that I don't ever do anything for me anymore. The last time I had a pedicure was right before New York. The last time I ate a meal that wasn't designed to make my kids happy **was** New York.*

Three months after New York, Maggie wrote:

Okay, good news is that I really do feel that I am learning to control my temper better. Last night when Mom was on my back about how she feels that the boys were up too late, I didn't get sarcastic or snarky, which was a big victory for me. The bad news is that I can't let go of how much I liked Andre and I spend hours each day thinking about what I should've done, could've done, and what might be now if I had handled it better. Last night, I spent almost an hour online, on his firm's website, just staring at pictures of him. How lame is that? I can't seem to let go of the fantasy.

Four months after New York, Kim arrived for a long weekend. After hugging the shrieking boys and sending them off to find gifts in her car, she looked Maggie over carefully. "Hey baby sister, you look like shit."

"Nice to see you, too." Maggie's voice rose defensively.

Kim swatted her playfully on the arm, "Oh, don't get all pissy on me. You do look like hell. Even worse, you look like you don't even care." Her words were softened by her hug. "But, we'll work on all of this over the weekend. By Monday, you'll be ready for the Ms. America competition, and more importantly, you'll be out of this funk you're in. Time to get your head outta your ass."

The next morning, Maggie woke to find Kim already in the kitchen with a legal pad full of notes, a steaming mug of black coffee next to the pad. "Here's the plan, Mags. This morning you have a hair appointment at ten, and then we're heading to Burlington to shop. Mike will watch the boys. After that, we're coming home, taking the kids, and meeting Devon and Mike at the Gazebo Festival to hear the Arcadian band. And you're even going to wear some makeup tonight." Kim's tone was matter of fact and reminded Maggie why she was able to command a full staff of junior executives without breaking a sweat.

"And if I don't want to get my hair done and wear makeup?"

"Truly? Right now, I don't give a flying shit for what you think you want. You'll do it or else."

"Or else what?"

"I'll tell Mom."

Maggie's eyes widened. "You wouldn't! She doesn't know a thing about this, and if she found out, I'd never hear the end of it."

"I know. That's why I used that as a threat." Kim squeezed Maggie's hand, "I've watched you slide deeper and deeper into the pit of despair, and I let you have time to work it out on your own. You've spent the last few months sitting here beating yourself up for allowing yourself some fun. You've spent months waiting for the phone to ring or mail to arrive, and nothing is coming, pumpkin. Just to remind you, you chose to leave him without any contact info. He's not going to magically appear in your kitchen. You have to accept that it's over. You've cried a friggin' ocean and eaten Ben & Jerry's until they're about to name their next flavor after you. By the way, Devon and Mike call constantly, because they're worried about you. Now it's time for me to give you a swift kick in the ass, a kiss on the cheek, and send you back out into the world. It's done."

Maggie tried not to get angry at her sister's truthful words. "I know." She sighed, and straightened her shoulders, "Okay, I'll try your way today."

"Great. That's all I want."

That evening, Maggie stood in her room looking in the mirror. Kim sat on the bed behind her, glowing with self-satisfaction. "I told you; you look amazing. You should have cut your hair ages ago. And the dress suits you."

Maggie twisted around, admiring herself in the bright sundress, perfect for the summer weather. Her hair barely covered her ears, and with the new cut, it waved wildly. "I admit it. I do love it."

"Good. Now let's go to the concert."

The whole town apparently decided to attend the Gazebo Festival. Maggie and Kim carried the picnic baskets, while Mike and Devon each carried a boy on their shoulders.

Finding space to spread the blankets, the six of them sat down. Passing Devon a soda, Maggie smiled at him, "I'm really sorry Claire couldn't come with us tonight. I like her, Dev, and I'm really glad you're dating again."

Devon shrugged, his brown eyes reflecting a lasting sadness. "I still wake up every morning wishing Mary Anne was here, and Claire knows that. But Mary Anne isn't coming back, and I guess four years is long enough to try to accept the concept. Claire is a lot of fun, and she's not pressuring me." He poked Mike in the ribs, "What about you? Who's the flavor of the month?"

Mike laughed, his shaggy blond hair glinting in the streetlights. "I seem to be out of flavors right now." He turned to Kim, raising one eyebrow, "Besides, we all know deep down, I'm in love with Kim; I'm just waiting patiently for her to realize she loves me. Then we'll get married and live in over-sexed bliss forever."

Kim shook her head, rolling her eyes. "Waiting patiently? Sweetie, you need a full-time administrative assistant just to keep track of the women you dated while you've been so-called *waiting*."

The group settled comfortably, listening to the music as the sky darkened. The boys curled up on the blanket and Nick fell asleep. Maggie relaxed, and realized she felt better than she had since New York.

Kim leaned over, "Hey, Mags. There's a really hot guy over there that keeps checking you out."

"Where?"

"By the statue of Emma Willard."

Slyly, Maggie looked quickly toward the statue. Her eyes widened as she whispered to Kim, "That's Javier, the new Spanish professor at the college. I spoke with him quickly after a union meeting last month. He seemed nice."

Kim nudged her—hard. "Dummy! I'm not noticing his personality right now. Look at those eyes!" She leaned closer so she could get a better view, "Look at his butt! I could take a bite out of it, it's so perfect. Get your ass off the blanket and go walk over that way. Go to the garbage can or get a program or something. Walk by him and say hi. You know, like you just noticed he's here," she coached.

Maggie shook her head, "Kim, I don't want to go say hi to a guy. I'm still working this out in my mind, okay?"

Her voice was emphatic, "No. Not okay at all. I'm not saying go jump him, just say hello. It'd do you a world of good just to say hello to a man, especially one who looks like that."

Maggie shook her head. "Forget it. I'm not gonna do it."

"Your mistake." Her eyes sparkled, "I dare you," she started to laugh, "I *double-dog* dare you."

"I can't believe you're this immature!" Ten minutes later, Maggie stood up unexpectedly and grabbed a handful of wrappers. She leaned down to whisper in Kim's ear. "Fuck you, you win."

Kim's laughter rang in Maggie's ears as she crossed the park.

Walking toward the garbage cans, Maggie tried not to be obvious, knowing Javi was standing nearby, leaning against a tree. Dropping the wrappers in the can, she turned, a smile innocently plastered on her face, "Javi! I didn't see you there. How are you?"
Javi stepped forward, holding out his hand, "Maggie. So good to see you. I'm good."

"Enjoying the beautiful weather?"

"I am. Are you here with friends?"

"Friends, my sister, and my sons." Maggie swallowed, feeling awkward, "Would you like to come over and meet them?"

He smiled, "I'd love to."

That night, after everyone else was asleep, Maggie lay in bed with her journal. The next question was: *How are you changing the patterns of behavior? What seems to help, what seems to hinder your progress?* For a few moments, Maggie stared into space, thinking about the question. What an interesting coincidence today's assignment would be to answer those questions!

I guess what I would say is that frankly, since I returned from New York, most of what I've done is sit and mope because it didn't turn out like I hoped. Although I can say I've been better about thinking before I speak most of the time and haven't told anyone off in a long while. Other than that, I haven't changed much of anything. My sister is here for a visit, and she pointed out I need to change my behavior. She made me get a haircut and go out tonight. It helped make me feel more optimistic about life in general. What helps? Being on vacation means my schedule is lighter, which definitely helps me keep my temper under control. What hinders? Me. I hinder myself. When I'm down, I can't get out of my own way. I guess that's what Kim was trying to get me to see. Tonight, Kim dared me to go over near a guy I know from work, who seemed to be looking at me. I did it, reluctantly, but I did go, and ended up talking to him, and he then came over and sat with us for the rest of the concert. I guess I have to accept that the thing with Andre is done, and I need to go forward.

The next afternoon, Maggie sat in her office at the college, enjoying a few minutes of catching up on email while Kim took the boys to the lake. Suddenly, she heard a noise in the hallway, becoming hyper-aware of the sound of someone approaching. The building was locked! Who was here, and why? She stood up, bracing herself defensively, years of self-defense training foremost in her mind. Suddenly, the doorknob to her office turned, and a heavily accented voice called out, "Maggie, are you here?"

Recognizing the voice, Maggie tried to calm her racing heart, "Javi! What are you doing here?"

Striding into her office, he clearly didn't notice how agitated she was. "I saw your car outside, so the custodian let me in."

Trying to sound normal, Maggie stammered, "Oh, great." She tried to smile, "C'mon in."

"May I sit down?"

Maggie motioned to one of the battered chairs across from her desk, "Of course."

Over the next ten minutes, Javi chatted about his new teaching role, his office, moving to Vermont, and missing Spain. Maggie thought she sounded relatively intelligent by the time they discussed Spain, telling him about her grandfather, the matador.

Finally, Javi stood up. "I should let you get back to work." He paused in the doorway, "Would you go out with me sometime? Dinner or drinks?"

In her heart, Maggie knew she didn't want to go out with anyone but Andre, but that was impossible. Javi was nice, smart, and gorgeous. "Sure, drinks would be great."

"How about tomorrow night? I'll pick you up around eight and we can go to Two Brothers?"

"How about I meet you there? See you at eight."

"See you then."

That night, Maggie lay in bed, the TV on, and started to write,

So, I did it, I accepted a date with the guy from the concert. His name is Javi, and he's a professor at the college. I can't say I really want to go out with him, because, yes, as stupid, and pathetic as it sounds, I keep hoping it will magically work out with Andre, but I need to accept it isn't going to. Javi is attractive, nice, smart, and no matter what, it won't hurt me to go out with him for drinks.

Chapter Thirteen

Three weeks later, Maggie held the cordless phone on her shoulder as she folded laundry. "Hey, Kim, it's me."

"Hey, baby sister. How the heck are you?"

"Pretty good. I had my last session last night, and I graduated. Dr. Robinson reported I've learned to control my temper, and I will act like an amazingly well-adjusted individual from now on."

Kim laughed, "No he didn't!"

"You're right, he didn't. He told me I did what was necessary to graduate and keep my job, and I need to think before I spout off at Dean Anderson again."

"That sounds more like it. How's your love life?"

"It's going okay."

"Okay? Hello? Details!"

Maggie thought for a second, "Javier really is a nice guy and we've gone out, I guess, about seven times. A couple movies, took the boys to the fair, we and went to see a Hispanic chamber concert. He's had dinner here a few times."

"Your tone isn't exactly gushing. Do you like him?"

"Yeah. I mean it's really different. I guess that since I was so head-over-heels in New York, I was hoping this would make me feel the same way, but it doesn't. It's very comfortable. He's nice, funny, likes the boys, and is kind…"

"Damn. You make it sound like those are bad things, what's the problem?" Kim sounded deflated.

"You know how Mom always wants Dad to dress up for dinner, to not wear jeans at the table, that kind of stuff?"

"What do Mom and Dad have to do with it? Good Lord, talking about *them* in conjunction with your love life makes me queasy."

"Well, he's like Mom. We have a lot of fun, but he's come for dinner twice, and each time he's offered to watch the food while I change for dinner. Like he's basically thinking my choice of clothes isn't appropriate for dinner. When I don't change, he seems somewhat put off. And he's always wearing nice clothes. Dressing up like that isn't me. You know, I dress up for work, but at home, I'm happy in my jeans. He insists on paying when we go out, even though I know I make more than he does. So, I wish he'd let me pay for the boys sometimes, stuff like that. Chivalry is great, but sometimes I feel like he's either trying to change me or buy me."

"Let me get this straight, you're bitching because he dresses well and pays for you? Damn, honey, most women would kill themselves out of despair in such a situation. How's the sex?"

Maggie laughed, realizing how whiny she sounded. "I have no clue. We're just in the kissing stage."

"Seriously? After three weeks, all you're doing is *kissing*? And?"

"And… he's a good kisser. Maybe not as assertive as he could be, but I think he's trying to give me time."

"Well tell him to hurry the hell up and put some effort into it."

"I don't know if I want him to."

"What do you mean?"

"Well, remember when Mom would make flan?"

Kim snapped, "Jesus, Mags, what the hell is it with you today, mentioning our parents when we're talking about your love life?"

"Hear me out! Remember the flan?"

"Of course!"

"Well, remember the caramel syrup?"

Kim sounded completely exasperated. "Of course, I do. You'd cry if the boys poured off your syrup before you got to it, leaving you with just the custard. They did it just to piss you off and you fell for it every time."

"Because the custard alone was boring. I hate plain custard but love flan with the syrup."

"What the fuck does flan have to do with Javi?"

"He's like the custard. He's sweet and nice, but I want the damn syrup. He's like plain old vanilla custard."

Kim started to laugh, "I can't believe you just referred to your boyfriend as plain old vanilla custard! So put some damn syrup on him!"

Maggie laughed. "Anyway, he's coming to dinner tonight. Devon, Claire, Mike and some old friend of Devon's are coming too."

"Wow, you invited him to eat with Devon and Mike? That's like a sacred invitation. He may be vanilla custard, but you like him enough to invite him into the inner sanctum."

Maggie chuckled, "Yeah, yeah."

"So, Mike's back?"

"Yeah. He got back last night."

"What are the boys up to?"

"I'm going to feed them frozen pizza..."

"Their favorite."

"You know it. They're going to eat in just a few minutes and watch television while the adults eat. They're so excited about Jake coming, they can't see straight."

"I can't remember what you said, when does he arrive?"

"The day after tomorrow. He should be here mid-day to pack them up, then off they'll go for the week." Maggie looked at her watch. "Shit, I didn't realize it was so late. Javier will be here in an hour, the rest soon after. I have to run. Love you."

"Love you too. If anything interesting happens tonight, call me after they leave."

Chapter Fourteen

The windows were ablaze with light as Devon drove up the driveway. "Well, we're here."

Claire turned around in the front seat to face their passenger. "Andre, you'll love everyone. We get together once a month for dinner like this. It'll give you a chance to meet a few people, so maybe you'll see a familiar face at the grocery store or something."

Andre smiled, "Sounds great, I appreciate the invitation. Sitting at the hotel alone tonight didn't sound terribly appealing."

"Sorry about the painters taking so long, the apartment will be ready tomorrow morning," Devon apologized. "We'll help you move stuff if you want."

"If you don't mind, that would be wonderful." Andre grinned, "Besides, I think I moved you twice back in Washington."

"At least twice! And one of them was on the top floor."

"I remember it well!"

Devon parked in front of a white house. As Andre exited the car, he paused to admire the bright flowers overflowing their beds on both sides of the driveway.

A board creaked loudly as he crossed the porch behind Devon and Claire, barely audible over the music pouring through the open front door.

"Jaded," was playing so loudly, Devon needed more force into his knock, rattling the screen door on its hinges. "She *does* love Aerosmith." When no one appeared, he knocked again, calling out loudly, "Hello?"

Seconds later, a small blond boy appeared at the screen door, a huge smile spreading across his face as he recognized the visitors. "Uncle Devon! Yay, Mommy told us you'd be here." He unlocked and opened the screen door for them. "Hi, Claire."

Claire leaned down to hug the small boy, "Hey, Eli. Cool jammies."

The boy looked down proudly at his Harry Potter pajamas. "Mommy got them in New York," he said, then looked at Andre and frowned. "Hi. Who are you?"

Andre rubbed the back of his neck, always uncomfortable with the mannerisms of small children. "I'm Andre."

Devon ruffled the boy's hair, "Eli, Andre's an old friend of mine. He's going to eat dinner with us."

"Oh." The answer obviously satisfied him as he smiled at Andre. "You can come in."

Andre stepped into the hallway. Solemnly, the boy looked up at him and held out his hand. "My name is Eli. I'm five, but I'm gonna be six someday, and I want a really big Lego set for my birthday."

Feeling like Gulliver, Andre shook his small hand. "Andre Serapes. I'm thirty-six."

"Wow. You're old. I'm not going to be thirty-six for a hundred birthdays." Andre found himself charmed despite his discomfort. "Uncle Devon, Mommy is finishing Nicky's bath, and Javi's in the kitchen. I think he's making dinner or something."

As they entered the living room, Eli turned down the stereo, and Andre suddenly heard squeals of young laughter from upstairs.

Eli motioned toward a couch. "Mr. Andre, you can sit there, if you want to, or you can come in the kitchen."

Claire touched his sleeve, noticing Andre's discomfort. "Come on, Andre. Let's go in the kitchen, that's where we'll probably eat."

Feeling distinctly out of place, Andre followed Devon and Claire into the kitchen, thinking he should have stayed at the hotel tonight and settled into his apartment before meeting new people.

In the kitchen, a tall dark-haired man stood by the stove, stirring what seemed to be a pot of simmering tomato sauce. Hearing their footsteps, he turned. "Devon! And Claire, how nice to see you both again." His slight accent fit with his European clothing and mannerisms. He held out a hand to Andre, "I'm Javier Gonzalez, welcome."

"Andre Serapes. Thank you for inviting me. You have a beautiful home and a lovely son."

Javier chuckled, "Actually, I can't take credit for either. I'm a guest here tonight just like you. Somehow, I was appointed the sauce stirrer." He motioned toward a round oak table, with a basket of red geraniums in the center. "Please have a seat. There's an open bottle of wine there, or beer, seltzer, and soda in the refrigerator."

While Devon and Claire set out their cheese platter, Andre sat down warily. He noticed the light colors of the room and the comfortable furniture. A group of toy cars were neatly parked on the edge of the area rug. From upstairs he heard bits of conversation. "Olympics ... Britain ... Oh, no ... Russia ..."

Eli watched Andre and saw his confused look. "Mommy's giving Nicky his bath. She wanted to give him his bath earlier, but she got busy talking to Aunt Kim and forgot about the time. He's taking his bath now, and they're playing bath Olympics. If he's good, Mommy says he won the gold medal, but if he's bad, some other country wins."

He stood up. "I have to feed my cat." He picked up a cup of water and took a sip. "Andre, my cat's name is Jack, and he's a black cat."

"Oh."

"And Mommy will be right done… I mean down."

Devon went to the bottom of the stairs. "Hey, you home? We're here."

A muffled voice shouted, "Be right down."

Minutes later, as Andre sipped from a glass of wine, he heard footsteps descending the staircase. A feminine voice shouted, "Eli! Hey, Eli. Nicky won gold again!" There was no answer. "Eli! Remember, we need to brush your teeth before you can watch television, c'mon!"

Light footsteps ran toward the hall. "Okay, Mommy. Mommy, did you say hi to Uncle Devon and Claire and Andre?"

"Who?"

"Andre!" His young voice rose. "Uncle Devon's friend, Andre. He came to dinner with them. I let them in, cuz Javi was stirring dinner. Everybody's in the kitchen."

Although she was certain it couldn't be "her" Andre, Maggie still leapt toward the kitchen. Seeing Andre sitting calmly at her table, unaware of her entering the room, she stopped dead. All color drained from her face and her arms dropped, sending neat piles of laundry cascading from the loaded basket she carried.

All four adults in the kitchen turned. Andre's shocked eyes swept over her, recognition struggling with disbelief. A damp towel thrown over her shoulder echoed the wet spots on her t-shirt. Her long hair was gone, replaced by new wild waves. Her faded jeans were damp, and bright pink toenails sparkling from under their frayed hems. Both her jeans and t-shirt accentuated the amazing curves he still thought about longingly each night.

Andre stood up, staring intently as he catalogued all the changes from the woman he met in New York.

Maggie's cheeks burned as she tried to keep her voice neutral. "Andre."

Before he could respond, a smaller boy raced into the room, launching himself at Maggie. "I did it! I got my pajamas on all by myself!"

Maggie hugged him distractedly. Kissing the damp blond waves on the top of his head, her eyes never left

Andre. "Good job, Nick. Did you say hi to Uncle Devon and Claire?"

"No. I was just in the tub, remember?"

"Right. Well, say hi, and then go find Eli. You guys get your toothbrushes ready. I'll be there in a minute."

As the child raced away, Maggie looked hard at Andre's shocked face.

Finally, he spoke. "Maggie."

Devon stood up, completely confused. "Maggie. This is Andre. I didn't know you knew each other."

Javier moved to Maggie's side, possessively rubbing her arm as he bent to pick up the laundry. "Magita," his voice was concerned, "are you alright?"

The color rose again in Maggie's cheeks. *Now* Javier decided to be more assertive? "Thanks, Javi, I'm fine." She bent quickly, scooping laundry into the basket. "The basket just slipped out of my hands, that's all."

Devon was still mystified. "Maggie. This is Andre. Do you know each other?"

Andre's voice was calm, although Maggie could tell he was seething. "We met several months ago, at a conference." He held out his hand to Maggie, forcing her to take it. "How nice to see you again. And so *unexpectedly*."

Somehow, Maggie controlled her voice, shocked at the intensity of her emotions his touch evoked. What the heck was she supposed to say? How do you act around a guy you had a one-nighter with and then left? "Good to see you too, Andre."

Just then, the front door slammed, and a male voice sounded from the living room. "Hey, Buttercup, sorry I'm late; I had to run back to the hospital."

Andre froze, his eyes boring into Maggie's. Who was this? How the hell many men did she have in her life? Obviously, he knew nothing about Maggie.

Maggie's face turned bright red. "We're in the kitchen, Mike."

Together, Javier and Andre chimed, "Buttercup?"

Maggie sighed, "Oh, hell. It's a really stupid story. Come sit down and have a drink and meet each other while I get the boys settled. Somebody will explain."

A blond man strode into the kitchen. Hiking shorts clung to his muscular thighs, and his blue t-shirt emphasized broad shoulders and his narrow waist.

Andre instinctively clenched his fists.

Although the man's eyes widened to see strangers in the kitchen, he didn't comment. Instead, he looked at Maggie. "Sorry I'm late." He held out a bouquet of slightly bedraggled flowers. "I brought a peace offering."

Maggie laughed and kissed him on the cheek. "Heya, Mikey. Don't sweat it. You're not late. Devon and company just got here, and the boys are about to go watch some television so we can eat. By the way, welcome home."

She pulled the newcomer toward the two strangers. "Javier, Andre, this is Mike Sanders. Javi, you met him at the concert. He lives in the cottage on the back edge of the property. He's the head of the emergency department at the hospital."

"Mike, this is Javier Gonzalez and Andre Serapes. Javier teaches Spanish at the college, which I think I mentioned to you before, and Andre is a lawyer in Boston. Andre and I met in New York when I went to the conference. If you'll all excuse me a minute, I just need to get the boys settled." Maggie looked imploringly at Mike, hoping he wouldn't say anything stupid, considering she told him all about Andre in the days following her trip.

Mike shook hands with both men. "Nice to meet you both. Andre, are you here for a visit?"

"No, I'm renting an apartment from Devon for the semester while I teach at Vermont Law."

Maggie heard Andre's comment as she was walking up the stairs and for a moment, felt dizzy. Andre was going to be living here in town for the semester. What the hell was she going to do now?

Mike grinned, "Oh, you mean you're renting from the three of us. We own that property together. Devon does the rental agreements." He chuckled knowingly, "I guess you could say Maggie is your landlady. Give her a call day or night if you need anything."

Andre looked sharply at Mike, wondering if he imagined Mike stressed the word *night*.

Devon sensed an undercurrent, so he motioned everyone toward the table. "Come sit down. It looks like we may be eating on the deck, but we can wait for Maggie here. I'll pour drinks, and while I do that, Mike can explain the 'Buttercup' thing, so you don't think he's nuts."

Once Devon handed him a beer, Mike took a swig. "It's really pretty simple. When the four of us started college together, we lived in two of the three rooms of a freshman suite. The first day, Maggie's parents were helping her move in, and her father called her Buttercup. Dev and I thought it was pretty funny and it embarrassed the living hell out of Maggie that her dad kept calling her that in front of us. So, as a joke, we started using the nickname and it stuck. Now we just call her that to irritate her."

Devon shook his head, "No, you call her that more than I do. I've matured and found other ways to tick her off."

When Maggie returned, everyone was sitting at the table, chatting pleasantly.

Devon looked at her, "The guys settled?"

"Happy as can be, watching a Disney movie." She brushed a curl out of her eyes, "I thought we could eat on the deck, if you all want to help bring things out there."

Maggie avoided Andre as the group carried platters and beverages to a table on the back deck overlooking an oval swimming pool, and she was careful to put her glass of wine as far from his seat as possible.

Trying to appear relaxed, Andre sat at the table and made small talk with Claire. A group of candles glowed on the table, and Andre admired the comfortable feel of the area. A hammock stretched across one corner of the deck, the perfect spot overlooking the pool. Tucked into a corner of the deck, partially screened by latticework and hanging plants, was a small hot tub. Andre fought a brief surge of anger at the thought of her sitting in the steaming water with Javier.

Devon raised his glass, "A toast – to new friends and old ones, and to our hostess, who always manages to pull these things together so perfectly, and so calmly."

Maggie blushed, "You weren't here earlier today when I couldn't find the pasta pot; it turned up in the garden, serving as a turtle condo. I wouldn't want homeless turtles, so luckily, I found another pot in the basement."

Soon everyone was eating and talking. Maggie slipped into silence as she watched the group and picked at her dinner. Javier sat next to her, his arm around her chair for much of the meal. At one point, while people finished their meals, Javier stroked the back of her neck while he made a comment to Mike.

Shocked by the intimate touch, Maggie stiffened. As she sat straighter, her eyes met Andre's. From his seat at the far end of the table, he raised one eyebrow and then averted his eyes.

Maggie rose, "I'm going to put a pot of decaf on. I'll be right back."

Immediately, Javier rose. "I'll help you."

She lightly pushed his shoulder down. "No, you and Mike seem to be enjoying your conversation. I'm fine."

Mike grinned, having seen Javier's touch, Maggie's reaction, and Andre's look. "Hey, Andre. Maybe you could help Maggie in the kitchen while Javi and I finish our conversation about El Salvador. That would give you two a chance to catch up."

Maggie bared her teeth. "That's okay. Really, Andre, I don't need any help."

Andre suddenly wanted to make her feel as uncomfortable as he did. "I don't mind. Besides, I'd love to hear about your summer, you know, *after* your trip to New York."

Chapter Fifteen

By the time Andre reached the kitchen, Maggie had her back to him, carefully measuring coffee into the machine. He might have believed she didn't know he was there, or care, except for the shaking of her hands.

He cleared his throat, torn between wanting to kiss her senseless and wanting to drown her with his hurt and anger. "So..."

Maggie swallowed, her back still toward him. "So..."

"Look at me."

Avoidance seemed like a good idea. "I have to pay attention to this right now."

Andre stalked across the kitchen, and stopped so close behind her she felt his body heat. "No, you don't. Forget the damn coffee. Look at me."

Maggie turned but couldn't look at him. "Andre, you have to believe me, I didn't know…"

"Bullshit. I don't have to believe you. Look at me, damn it." Reluctantly, she looked up at him, and he saw the nervousness in her eyes, but his anger was too great. "Did you have fun today, knowing you would have a good laugh at my expense? You know, I profess my devotion to you in New York, then you run away, and now I'm here, signing a teaching contract and a fucking lease, and to top it all off, you're my *landlady*?"

Shock washed over Maggie when she realized he thought she set him up. "Andre, I didn't know you were coming today. Honest. You saw my reaction; I was as shocked as you. I didn't set this up."

"Honest? You want me to accept your word as truth now? In the time I've known you, I made an ass of myself chasing after you, got left behind when you took off – with no explanation may I add, and then I walk in tonight to have dinner with strangers, and find you being pawed by another man."

"He's not pawing me! He touched my arm, that's it."

"Bullshit, and you know it! He's marking his territory, pure and simple. Even he knew something was off between us, and he's making sure I damn well know you're with him."

"You're imagining things!"

"I am not." He stepped closer, pressing her back into the counter. Even with his anger, Maggie felt herself responding physically to his touch. "Are you *his*? Does he make you feel like I did?"

Maggie felt anger surge through her, even as her body responded to his words, and she pushed his chest away, but he didn't budge, "I'm not his anything. As for how he makes me feel, that's none of your damn business."

"It is and you know it. No matter how it ended, both of us still felt something when we saw each other tonight." He leaned even closer, hissing through his teeth. "And if he touches you again while I'm around, I may just kill him. I may not be able to be with you, but I'll be damned if I'll watch another man hang all over you."

Chapter Sixteen

As Maggie tried to think of a response, she heard footsteps approach. Andre quickly stepped away, all expression draining from his face.

Mike and Devon entered the room, each carrying a pile of dirty dishes. They set them in the sink as Maggie moved to stack them in the dishwasher. Just as they started back toward the deck, the phone rang. "Mike, please get the phone, my hands are full."

"Hello, Maggie's house." Mike obviously recognized the voice on the other end of the line. "Hi, Mrs. Erickson, how are you?"

Maggie rolled her eyes, fighting an urge to scream. Mike poked her in the arm, grinning, and Maggie muttered, "Great, this is just perfect, a call from Mom is *exactly* what I need right now."

He smirked, "Hold on Mrs. Erickson, I'll get her. She's just rinsing some dishes."

As Mike handed her the phone, Maggie kicked him in the shin, "Thanks for mentioning the dishes, you asshole." Grimacing, she picked up the phone, "Hi, Mom. Yes, Mom. I'm making sure there isn't *any* food left on the dishes before I put them in the dishwasher. Yes, Mom." She sighed, oblivious to everyone watching her. "Yes, Mom. I know the dishwasher runs more efficiently if the dishes are well rinsed, that's why I completely wash them by hand first, just like you do. No, Mom, I'm sorry, I wasn't giving you an attitude, never mind, forget I said anything."

Someone knocked on the front door. "Mom, hold on, someone's here." Holding her hand over the phone, Maggie hissed, "Someone please get the door and hand me my gun so I can shoot myself, since I am definitely a failure as a daughter because my dishes aren't clean enough for the dishwasher." She sighed.

Devon squeezed her arm comfortingly and walked out of the kitchen, "I'll get the door."

Andre's eyes narrowed as Maggie returned her attention to the telephone. Just then, Devon walked back into the room with a bemused look. "Mags!"

Maggie snapped. "What, Dev? I'm on the phone!"

"Mags, Jake's here."

Chapter Seventeen

Andre watched as Maggie's face showed complete disbelief. Who was Jake? Damn, how many men *were* in her life? "Dev, that's not funny. Jake is *not* here. He won't be here until the day after tomorrow."

Devon shook his head, his eyes wide. "Mags, Jake's here. He just ran back out to the car to grab something."

Cutting her mother off in mid-sentence, Maggie barked, "Mom, I have to go, Jake's here." She swallowed, visibly angry at her mother's response. "I don't know why he's here, but I'll be sure to tell him how much you miss him. Goodbye, Mom."

Behind Devon, a tall blond man strode into the kitchen. Wearing chinos and a simple button-down shirt, he walked into the room exuding confidence, clearly comfortable in Maggie's house.

Maggie stared at him, her face stony, as Devon and Mike moved to stand on either side of her.

Jake smiled, bemused, "I see you still have your loyal bodyguards." He swallowed, "Mike, Dev, good to see you again." Jake looked around the room at the other faces, and then turned toward Maggie and flashed an apologetic grin. "Hi, Mags. I didn't know you had people over."

"You would've if you bothered to call first, you know, like it says in the paperwork you signed? You said you'd be here the day after tomorrow, so what the hell are you doing here now?"

"My leave got extended. I'm sorry if you're mad, but I wanted to see the guys so badly."

Understanding flowed through Andre. This was her ex-husband. Could the evening get any stranger?

Maggie shook her head resignedly, "Fine. You're here now." Stepping forward, she kissed his cheek, "You ass, you should have called."

"I know."

She gestured toward the kitchen table, still laden with food. "Did you eat?"

"No. It's okay, I can get something in town."

"Don't be a shithead, there's plenty." She looked around, "Jake, this is Andre and Javi and Claire, everyone, this is Jake, the boys' dad." She motioned toward the serving dishes, "Fix yourself a plate while I get the boys."

"Okay."

Maggie walked to the stairs, and called up, "Nick, Eli, come here. I have a surprise for you!"

"But Mommy, it's the *good* part of the movie!" Eli whined.

She smiled and looked over at Jake. "I think you'll really like the surprise, hurry down!"

Thirty seconds later, the boys bounded down the stairs. As Eli rounded the corner, he saw his dad leaning against the door frame and he froze, Nick almost colliding with him. "Daddy? Daddy!" he exclaimed in disbelief.

Andre watched in amazement as the little boy burst into tears and launched himself into his father's arms, Nick following right behind. Jake picked up both boys, kissing them, telling them how much he loved them.

Within ten minutes, the boys had settled on their father's lap as he ate his dinner, and the rest of the group ate dessert. Once he finished eating, Jake and the boys climbed into the hammock, cuddling, Nick dozing on and off.

Andre marveled at the staggering resemblance between Jake and his sons. They must be a daily reminder to Maggie of her ex-husband – did she wish she were still married to him?

While the group chatted, Andre watched how carefully Maggie sat so Javi couldn't touch her, and he could see Javi's frustration growing by the minute. Finally, Devon stretched, "I guess we should be going."

Maggie stood up. "Help me bring this stuff into the kitchen. I'll take care of it in the morning."

Javi put his hand on her back possessively, "I'll help you clean up tonight."

"No, Javi. Thanks so much. At this point, I'll just leave it and get some sleep. It's been a long day." Andre tried to keep his face straight when Javi's face registered anger and disappointment.

"Okay then."

Minutes later, the group stood at the door. Claire hugged and kissed Maggie, "Great dinner, Maggie. Talk to you soon?"

Devon and Mike each hugged Maggie, yelled goodbye to Jake, and headed toward their cars. Andre stopped in front of Maggie, "Thank you for dinner."

"You're welcome."

Javi came up behind her, put an arm around her, and said, "Thanks for joining *us* tonight, Andre. Hope your semester goes well."

"Thanks."

As Andre walked down the steps, he heard Javi ask Maggie, "Do you want me to stay now that Jake's here?"

"Jake stays here a lot. I'm fine. I'll talk to you tomorrow."

"Are you sure?"

Maggie sighed, "I'm sure. *Buenas noches*, Javi."

Thirty minutes later, Jake tucked the boys into bed, promising to make pancakes for breakfast. He walked downstairs to find Maggie sitting warily on the steps of the deck.

As soon as he came out on the deck, she demanded, "Now tell me the truth about why you're here early."

Jake sighed, "You always did believe in cutting to the chase. Can't you just accept I have extra time and I wanted to be with the boys?"

"I know you want extra time with the boys. What I don't get is why you *have* extra time. The United States military doesn't usually just hand out extra vacation time."

He smiled, knowing she was right, surprised she hadn't figured it out yet, "I'm being deployed. I got extra leave to make sure everything's in order before I go. And I was telling the truth, I had to get here as fast as I could because I wanted every single minute possible with them." He touched her arm. "I didn't mean to fuck up your party."

This news rocked Maggie. "I know you didn't. When?"

"Sixteen days from now."

"Where?"

"Flying over Syria or that region."

"Shit. Oh, Jake. Shit. I don't know what to say." Her voice cracked. "I just reached a point where I didn't think you'd have to go. You haven't deployed since we had kids. This feels so different."

"I know. That's how I feel too. But I am, and we need to spend time tomorrow going over arrangements. You know, like my will, wishes, that sort of stuff, just in case."

"Okay."

Jake tried to sound more relaxed. "It'll be okay, Mags. I'll go fly there for a while, buy you guys some cool gifts, and come home. And maybe after all of that, maybe I'll get stationed closer to you guys. You know, so maybe I could see Eli and Nick more often."

"They'd love that."

Jake stood up, "I'm getting something to drink. Do you want anything?"

"Shit, after tonight, a beer, please."

When he came back, he sat so he was facing her. "Okay, we'll deal with all of that tomorrow." He grinned. "I always forget when I'm away from you how there's never a dull moment when you're around."

"What do you mean by that?"

"Well, putting it bluntly, there were five men on this deck tonight. Devon is falling in love with Claire, Mike has the hots for Kim, or so he says. And then there were three others, counting me. Two of us had sex with you, and one wants to, and to make it really interesting, the one who wants to, but hasn't, is the guy you're dating."

"How the hell do you know that?"

"Mags, I'd have to be dumb or dead to not know. Javi wants you but can't figure out how to make it happen because he's a nice guy. Now, Andre, he's been to bed with you, and would kill to go back, but for whatever reason, he also was seriously pissed off. What the hell did you do?"

Maggie decided she had no reason to lie. "Remember how I told you I was going to New York for a conference?"

"Yeah, some dull thing about educational law."

"That's the one. I met Andre there, and had a …"

"You had a fling?" Jake started to laugh, "Oh, how the honorable have fallen!"

"Shut up. Anyway, we did, and then I found out that he was married before and really didn't, and *doesn't*, want children, won't even consider discussing the subject. I didn't tell him about the boys, and I couldn't tell him once he stated—unequivocally—he didn't want kids. So, I took off."

"Like, you took off without explaining why?"

"Yeah. I left his room, went to mine, grabbed my stuff, got a cab, and went to the airport. I left him a note saying something came up."

"And he didn't contact you again?"

"He couldn't."

Jake nodded, "Because of, as Mike always puts it, your privacy settings."

"Yeah. Unless you know how to look for me, you know I don't leave a digital footprint. I don't know if he tried to find me or not, but even if he did, with what Neil did for my security settings, it would make it almost impossible to find me."

"So, he thinks you just dumped him?"

"Yeah. And then he showed up tonight, completely out of the blue, because unbeknownst to me, he's friends with Devon from law school. By the time Dev was in law school, we were in Mississippi, so I didn't know his friends there. I never would've gotten the connection."

Jake nodded. "And then he showed up here."

"Uh-huh. Now he's living in one of our apartments and will be teaching at the law school."

"That's either the best or worst luck ever." He gulped his drink. "And you started dating Javi, when? It can't be too long ago."

"It wasn't. After New York, I fell into a slump. Then Kim came down and kicked me in the ass, we went to a concert, and I saw Javi there. He showed up at school the next day and asked me out."

For a moment, Jake was distracted by something in that last sentence. "He showed up at your school building? Were you alone?"

Maggie felt a moment of fondness that even after all they'd been through, Jake still cared intensely about her safety. "I was alone. The boys were with Kim. I just ran over to check messages, and he got a custodian to let him into the building. Almost scared me half to death when I realized he was in the building with me."

Jake shook his head, "That, I don't like. I thought the custodians all knew not to let anyone in without telling you first."

"They do. We just needed to re-up on that meaning known members of the faculty and staff too. They thought it was just for unknowns." She smiled. "It's okay, Jake. Really."

He took a sip, "Okay, but before I leave next week, I'm double-checking the system and your handgun, and you *are* going to the range with me."

A flash of irritation filled her as she wanted to argue with Jake about his right to order her to do anything, but that passed as soon as it arose. "Of course."

"Back to the story. So, you started dating Javi…"

"Yeah, I started dating Javi a few weeks ago."

"And it's a passionate, hormone-filled fantasy relationship?"

She rubbed the cold bottle on her forehead, "No, it's comfortable, moving along, probably really good for the boys, or at least I told myself that, and now all of this happened. And I don't have a friggin clue what to do about any of it."

"Mags, listen to me. Javi seems like a nice guy, and he seemed good enough around the boys, but he's not right for you."

"How do you know? And what business is it of yours?"

"Number one, you are the mother of my children, and what happens in your life impacts them, so I'll always care about that."

"Point taken."

"Mags, Javi would be a fucking lap dog for you. He'd do exactly as you told him. He was happy helping you pour coffee for everyone, for God's sake."

Maggie snorted in disbelief. "What the hell do you mean by that?"

"He's *dull*. He's a pretty boy. He spent more money on his hair cut than you did. His nails are manicured. Your nails look like you were weeding the garden this morning. You'd have to start wearing gloves when you're working outside, start dressing better, and put up with his constant politeness. Is that what you want?"

In her heart, Maggie heard the echoes of her earlier conversation with Kim. His accuracy irritated her further, and she reached the end of her patience. "Good night, Jake. Thanks for the advice. I really need advice from *you*."

Jake grabbed her hand as she started to walk away. "Mags, I have nothing to gain by saying it, remember that. And truly, I want you to be happy."

The next morning, after a breakfast of pancakes and lakes of maple syrup, Maggie sent the boys to clean their rooms while she and Jake sat at the kitchen table.

He opened a manila envelope. "All of my papers are here. I filed all of them with my lawyer as well, but I wanted you to have a copy in advance. Everything still goes to you, so you can take care of the boys."

Maggie's eyes filled with tears. "Damn, Jake. Shut up. Nothing is going to happen to you and now you're making me cry."

A few hours later, the boys were snugly strapped in their car seats. Maggie kissed them goodbye one more time, then stepped back from the car. "Take care of them. And my phone is always on if you need to reach me."

"I know. And you can call anytime you want. We'll be back in a week."

Chapter Eighteen

The next night, Maggie packed her picnic basket sullenly, then sat down with her journal, and muttered, "I can't believe I'm still using this stupid journal after I graduated from the program."

So last night Andre showed up at my house because he's moved here. He didn't know he was going to see me; I didn't know I was going to see him, and I sure as hell wouldn't have planned to have Andre and Javi meet each other. Then, to top the evening off, Jake showed up early because he's being deployed. All in all, it was a hell of a night! Now, I need to figure out what I'm doing with Javi, how Andre fits in all of this, and how I will take care of the boys while Jake is deployed.

Maggie put the journal down, and looked at her cell phone, reading Javi's text again with growing irritation. She still couldn't believe Javi cancelled their evening at the last minute by text message because he supposedly wasn't feeling well. Deep down, she knew he was sulking because she didn't ask him to stay after the dinner party. She was so glad Mike was able to go – how embarrassing it would be to go alone, especially since Andre would be there.

Mike walked into the kitchen unannounced, startling her. "You ready?"

"Yes. Grab the blanket, will you?"

At the concert site, Mike quickly spotted Devon and Claire, grinning when he saw Andre. "Oh, and look, Mags, Andre's here, and he doesn't have a date, either."

"I have a date, remember? You're it."

"No, Buttercup, I'm just your chauffeur. Remember the rules. We don't *ever* date each other."

The group quickly spread their picnic and settled back to enjoy the food. Maggie tried not to notice what Andre was doing, or if he seemed interested in her presence.

Devon passed Maggie a glass of wine. "So, what was up with Jake? It isn't like him to show up unexpectedly."

Maggie shook her head, her voice wry. "No, you're right. He just found out he's headed to a warm, dry climate for a while."

"Huh?"

For a moment, Maggie remembered her dear friends hadn't grown up on bases with parents being deployed, so they wouldn't understand her flip comment. "He's being *deployed*, so his leave was extended, and he came here to spend the extra time with the boys."

Devon's voice was deep with concern, "Oh, Mags. I'm sorry, that had to really suck for you. How'd the boys take the news?"

"Pretty well. Eli understands more what it means; Nick wanted to know if Jake could still call them."

"And you? How are you taking it?"

Andre sat to the side of the blanket, silently watching Maggie's reaction.

She shook her head. "It's not a picnic. Jake and I manage to be civil most of the time, friends sometimes, but somehow, talking with him about his last wishes felt really odd. We ended up joking about it because we were both so uncomfortable."

The concert started and the group relaxed companionably. At intermission, Mike and Maggie walked to the back edge of the property to look over

Lake Champlain. "Maggie, if the tension gets any higher between you and Andre, the whole place may go up in flames. You need to talk this out."

Maggie shook her head vehemently. "He thinks I'm a liar and I set him up. He thinks I knew about his friendship with Devon, and that I arranged for him to move up here."

Mike draped his arm around her shoulders, "Then you better figure out how to be around each other without the tension, because he's going to be here for the next six months. Otherwise, it's going to blow up in your face at the worst possible moment."

A few minutes later, Mike's hospital pager vibrated. Moving silently to the edge of the concert grounds, he called his service. When he came back, he crouched down to whisper in Maggie's ear, "Mags, I have to go. They need a surgeon right now and I'm closest. Can you get a ride with Devon?"

Maggie shrugged, "I'm sure I can. Go, it'll be fine."

Mike quickly left, and Maggie didn't have a chance to speak to Devon until the concert ended. "Dev, can I ride home with you guys?"

Devon looked uncomfortable. "Oh, Mags, we're not going back to town tonight. We're going to a wedding tomorrow in Burlington, so we decided to stay at the Radisson tonight."

Maggie was so stressed the past two days; she completely forgot Claire mentioning their plans. Before she could think of a response, Andre quietly offered, "I'll give you a ride."

Maggie's eyes widened, "Really?"

His voice was cold. "I'm headed back to town. It would be stupid for them to make a long trip out of the way."

If Maggie hadn't already felt uncomfortable, now she felt like a leper. "Thanks."

In the car, Andre quickly turned on a classical music station, drowning out any possible conversation. He didn't turn it down until they reached the town line. "Is there a shorter way to get there? Devon was coming from the other side of town the other night."

In other words, how could he get rid of her as soon as possible? Maggie pointed out the shortcut. Once at her house, Andre killed the engine.

Maggie cleared her throat, her mouth suddenly dry. "Thank you for the ride."

"You're welcome."

Maggie took a deep breath, Mike and Jake's earlier words echoing in her mind. "Andre, would you come in? So, we could talk?"

"Why?"

"Please, Andre. Couldn't we just talk for a few minutes with no one around to interrupt us?"

Andre sat in complete silence for what seemed an eternity before he opened the car door.

Inside, he stood woodenly in the hallway, "Okay, it's your dime, talk."

Maggie felt desperate, her bottom lip trembling. "Andre, please. Will you let me explain?" She stepped toward him, "Please?"

Maggie pressed her lips together, waiting for Andre's answer.

He sighed, "Fine."

"Thank you." She shrugged nervously, then cleared her throat. "Would you like something to drink? I have seltzer, wine, beer, soda, juice."

"A beer would be fine."

Moments later, Maggie reentered the room carrying two beers. She motioned toward the back door. "Do you want to sit outside?"

The floorboards creaked as they moved toward the two rocking chairs in the shadows of the deck.

Maggie handed Andre a beer. Sitting in the adjoining chair, she rocked nervously as she sucked in a long pull of her beer.

Turning the bottle in his hands, Andre felt the condensation wet his fingertips. In the dusky light, Maggie's green eyes looked anxious.

Taking a swig, the icy beer chilled his throat. He tried to smile. "This isn't the way I pictured seeing you again. I had a million scenarios why you left without saying good-bye. Over the last weeks, my feelings changed. I was hurt, mad, worried, hopeful, every possible emotion. Then, when I decided I couldn't live without seeing you again, I tried again to find you. I tried really hard, even hired a private investigator—twice—but you aren't an easy woman to find. Then I decided you knew how to find me if you wanted to, and you obviously didn't want to, so I gave up. I accepted this job, thinking a change would be good for me. The whole time, I kept thinking about how you'd react if we ever found each other again, but I never expected this."

"Andre, I'm so sorry."

Andre's stomach clenched as he tried to keep his voice calm. "For what? For running away without any sort of an explanation, or for not telling me you have children?"

Maggie's eyes filled with tears. With an impatient snort, she wiped her eyes with the back of her hand. "I guess I'm sorry for it all."

"Why, Maggie? Why didn't you say good-bye? Why didn't you tell me? Didn't it mean anything to you?" His voice rose. Slamming the beer down on the arm of the chair, his voice broke. "Damn!"

Maggie shouted, "It meant everything to me!"

"How can you say that?"

"Because it's true! God! Andre, here I was, this tired, dried-up nobody from Vermont. I mean, I don't think I had a date in the last year before I met you. All I planned to do was go to the sessions, eat a few meals while they were still hot, and visit a few museums." She smiled ruefully, "And then I made a complete ass of myself in the lobby. I thought that was it until you stood next to my table in the restaurant. Suddenly, my week wasn't about the conference, it was about squeezing in every second I could with you." Rubbing her temple with one hand, she took a swallow. "And I admit; it started sort of as a fling. I was going to break out of my shell and live again. Then we got closer to each other, and I hoped it would last."

His voice caressed her. "So did I."

"I kept trying to find the right moment to tell you about the boys. I guess I probably knew deep down it wouldn't work between us. You're this cosmopolitan type of guy; happy in that world, and I had a hell of a time playing princess. Women from the conference who saw us together at the hotel even commented about it being like a fairy tale."

She shrugged, "But, I guess I'm really more of the peasant sort. As much fun as it was, I like my house in the hills, my garden, and eating ice cream from the carton while I watch *Modern Family*. I love being a soccer mom, racing around with my boys in tow. That's not your world. I guess I really knew it wouldn't work but kept holding on to the dream."

"But you never even talked about it, you just ran! How could you not even tell me about the boys? Or their father? How could you possibly know if that isn't my world —when you didn't share enough of yourself to see how I would react?"

Maggie ignored the last comment. "I told you I was divorced, which is true. Frankly, other than that quick conversation I initiated about whether or not you were, we didn't talk about that part of our lives."

He didn't respond. Maggie continued. "That seemed like the most important issue right then. I mean, we had just slept together, and I suddenly realized it might be good to clarify we weren't married. As for my marriage, Jake is their father and we divorced because he cheated on me. Not once, but many times. I was going to tell you about the boys, I really was, but then we were talking about being divorced and..." Maggie stopped, unwilling to go on.

Andre's anger wilted as he suddenly remembered the conversation. "And I told you I was happy my marriage dissolved before we had children."

She nodded sadly. "And I knew then I had to go."

"Damn, Maggie. Why didn't you at least tell me what was going on?"

Maggie got up and moved to the railing. She climbed up and leaned against the pillar, only her silhouette visible in the increasing darkness.

"Andre, it wasn't that simple. I never do anything risky. I had to work hard at getting up the nerve to go out with you, to sleep with you. You need to understand Jake was the first guy I ever really loved. We started dating my junior year in high school. Eventually we became lovers. I mean, I really never dated anyone else. My sister was the one who dated everyone; I just wanted stability."

She shrugged. "When Jake and I were a couple, I kept pressing the marriage issue. Finally, he proposed, and in hindsight, I know now he proposed to shut me up. We were married, except he kept having affairs." She turned toward Andre. "The thing is, Jake's a fine father. Even when he's away, he tries to always be part of their lives. But I tried to make him into a husband, and it didn't work, and I couldn't fix it. Then you sat in that bed and told me calmly that you didn't want kids, I knew I couldn't beg you to change your mind." She laughed, but the sound was harsh and cold. "Jake wanted kids but not me. You wanted me but not the kids."

Andre sat and considered his answer, still reeling. "So, you walked away? You never gave me the opportunity to think about whether or not it could work?"

"Andre! Can you honestly sit here and say what you saw the other night made you want to jump into a relationship with me and my boys? It's a package deal. Damn, Andre, what you saw was a *calm* night! No fights, tantrums, or blood. No one cried or threw up. And they went to bed without a problem. That's heaven in my world."

His voice cut through the night. "No. I can't say I'm ready to jump in. What I realized is I don't know you. I know bits and pieces, but that's it. You know, in New York, we talked so easily, I thought I knew you pretty well. Then I got here, and another man was touching you like you were his. All I could think about was hurting him, making sure he never touched you again. Then your ex-husband showed up and again, another man who was part of your life was in my face, and I couldn't do a damn thing about it."

He stood up and strode over to stand in front of her. With one firm finger, he lifted her chin. "But I do know that what happened between us in New York was real, and I don't want to walk away from it. I don't know if I can take on the whole package, but I do know I need to do this." His lips descended and Maggie whimpered with desire as the kiss deepened. His tongue stroked hers and she had to grasp his shirt to steady herself.

When he pulled back, he touched her cheek. "I have to go."

Maggie struggled to keep the begging note out of her voice. "Will you come back? I mean… to me? I mean, I'm going to be here all day tomorrow if you want to come back."

He closed his eyes for a moment and whispered, "I honestly don't know, Maggie. I really don't." He stepped aside, placed both hands on the porch railing, and stared blankly at the dark lawn. "A week ago, I missed you so much it was killing me, and I was sure if we ever found each other again, everything would be okay. Now I'm here and I should be rejoicing because we're living in the same town, yet…I'm not."

Maggie sat, her muscles trembling with tension, waiting for him to continue.

He looked at her, barely seeing her. "I look at you, and right now I see only shadows. I don't know anything about you. Everything is different now that I know about the boys."

"How can I help you trust me again?"

"I don't know, I really don't. In my heart of hearts, I desperately want all of this to be okay. To forget and go forward, but I don't know if I can."

Chapter Nineteen

Shortly after Andre left, the phone rang. "Hello."

"Hey, Mags. How's everything?"

"Hey, Jake. How'd your day go? The boys seemed thrilled when I spoke with them earlier."

Maggie heard the smile in Jake's voice. "We had an awesome day. You know, sometimes I forget when I'm away from them how much fun we have. Even the little things—like eating at McDonald's is fun."

"I know. I mean, I'm really glad you're having fun, but I miss them."

"Anyway, they're sleeping now, and I just wanted to thank you."

"For what?"

"They're awesome. I can't take credit for that, you're the one raising them."

Tears pooled in Maggie's eyes. "Thank you for saying that," she whispered.

"I mean it. They're smart and handsome and I know that's the genetic combination of the two of us, but they're kind, funny, and excited about life. You're the one doing that."

Now the tears spilled down her cheeks, "I try. I don't know how well I do sometimes, but I try."

"What do you mean by that?"

"I mean, sometimes I wonder what the hell I'm doing. Like, Nicky still has trouble peeing in the toilet, and I'm a girl, I can't teach him a whole lot about aiming. You were home when Eli was learning. Or the other day Eli asked if his penis was as big as other boys. How the hell am I supposed to know that?"

Jake laughed, "You tell him he's my son, so it's way bigger than other boys."

Maggie chuckled, "Yeah, yeah. But I mean it, sometimes I wonder how well I'm doing."

"Stop wondering. You're doing an amazing job, and I wanted to tell you that."

"Thanks, Jake."

"Good night, Mags."

"Night, Jake."

Chapter Twenty

Hanging up the phone, Maggie moped on the couch, pretending to watch television before she finally dragged herself up the stairs and climbed into bed.

She barely slept that night. Every time a car drove by, she tensed, hoping it would turn into her driveway. As the hours passed, she kept wondering what Andre was doing, and if he was thinking about her.

As the light finally spilled over the mountains, she got up and showered. In the kitchen, she started a pot of coffee. Reaching for a mug, she almost dropped it when the phone rang. She looked at the clock. It was barely six. "Hello?"

In his apartment, Andre took a deep breath, unsure of what to say. "Hi."

"Hi."

He cleared his throat. "How are you?"

"Fine." Her voice shook, "No. I'm not."

"Neither am I." He closed his eyes, wondering how things went so wrong. "I've been thinking."

"Yes?"

"I have an idea."

"Okay."

"I was thinking maybe we could get together today and talk. I mean we could *really* talk. Not just small talk."

"You mean like talk about who we are?"

"Yes."

Maggie felt a glimmer of hope. "That sounds great."

"Could I come over?"

An hour later, Maggie paced nervously around her kitchen. Everything was spotless. When tires crunched over the gravel in the driveway, her stomach rolled again. What was it about this guy that tied her intestines in knots? Pushing her hair back from her face, she took one last look in the small mirror on the wall. "You can do this. This is what you want. Stop acting like an idiot!"

At the front door, she hesitated. Should she open the door and wait on the porch, or just wait at the screen door? What was welcoming and what was desperate?

She opened the screen door and held it as Andre walked up the porch steps.

Today he was wearing black jeans and a light gray t-shirt. Tired lines etched their way around his mouth, but he still carried himself with power and grace. When he reached the door, he looked down at her, and smiled slightly. "Hi. I'm Andre Serapes. And you are…?"

"C'mon in." She led him to the kitchen. "Why don't we sit here? Would you like some coffee or something?"

"That'd be great." He sat at the oak table, noticing the gleaming counters and appliances. A row of colorful, mismatched mugs hung over a coffee maker. Maggie filled two mugs and carried them to the table before grabbing cream from the fridge. "You like cream, no sugar."

"That's right."

Andre picked up a mug, smiling at the familiar Escher design. He savored the warmth of the coffee. "Nice mug. Thank you for the coffee."

"You're welcome," Maggie said, as she stirred cream into her coffee. "You look tired."

"I am." He took a sip. "I spent the night trying to figure out what to do. I almost called you about fifty times." His smile was rueful, "I finally had your phone number from the rental agreement on the fridge."

Maggie ignored the last comment. "I wish you had. I was awake too."

Andre reached across the table to squeeze her hand where it lay next to her mug. "Here's the thing: I spent the night going back and forth between wanting to beat down your door and beg you to let me back into your life and walking away completely."

"Andre, you don't have to be 'let' back into my life. You never left, I did."

"You know what I mean."

"Yeah, I guess I do." Still holding his hand, Maggie took a deep breath. "What do we do now?"

"I guess I need to know who you are. I realized we spent hours together, and even though many of them were spent talking, much of it was pretty meaningless. It was really just a prelude to going to bed, because the chemistry was building to an explosive level." He paused to sip his coffee, "I realized I don't even know things like what Maggie is short for, and I need to know them, to be able to see if we can work this out."

Maggie's response popped out, "Depose me."

"What?"

"I don't mean literally depose me but ask all the questions you want." Her lip quivered. "Andre, I went to bed with you in New York thinking it was a temporary thing, but I realized almost right away I didn't *want* temporary. I know I should have told you more than I did. And you have to believe how sorry I am. I want to try, and if hammering me with questions will help, ask away."

"Okay." He scowled. "Why couldn't I find Maggie O'Brien listed anywhere?"

"Because I keep my professional and personal lives separate. I use Maggie O'Brien personally, but my maiden name, Erickson, for work."

"Why? Why keep them separate?" For a millisecond, Andre saw sadness and fear cross her face, "What the hell happened to you that you keep them separate?" Maggie shifted in her chair as he continued, "I've had clients do that, usually because of something that happened in their past." He paused, looking at her searchingly, "It can't be because of your ex, Maggie. What happened to you, who hurt you?"

Her voice was small. "I didn't get hurt, luckily, but someone *wanted* to hurt me."

"What?"

She rotated the mug in her hands, then suddenly stood up and went to the coffee machine, her back to him as she spoke in a small voice. "When I was doing my clinical internship, I worked in a psychiatric corrections hospital in Mississippi. A patient there became obsessed with me. The short version of the story is that he broke out of the hospital, went to his mom's house, and told her we were going to be married, and he snapped, killing her. He went to my apartment; thank God I was at work." She turned back around, and Andre saw the stress on her face as she returned to the table, "My neighbor realized something was wrong because she could hear country music, so she called me at work to say something was off. By then, the hospital realized he'd escaped, and the whole thing came to light."

"What happened to him?"

"He's serving a life sentence in a psychiatric prison."

"But you make sure that you're hard to find."

She nodded, "Yeah."

"Do you have a security system?" He looked around the room and noticed a sensor near each of the windows.

"Yeah. There's an alarm system throughout the house, and there's a verbal signal if I need help." She looked down at her hands, her stress clearly visible, "My brother is in the intelligence community and made sure I have a really good system here, and that I'm really, really hard to find online. Hopefully, he'll never get out of jail, but if he does, I'll be notified." She rubbed her forehead. "Until last winter, we had the best guard dog ever, Speckles, but after she died, I didn't have the heart to go through the whole training thing again."

"Shit, Maggie. I don't know what to say." He took her hand and squeezed it gently.

"It's okay. But that's why you couldn't find me. Professionally, I'm not Maggie O'Brien."

"What is Maggie short for?" Andre didn't realize how curt his voice sounded, still shaken by hearing about her past.

Maggie tried to keep her defensiveness in check. Pulling her hand away from him, she crossed her arms over her chest unconsciously. "Magdalena."

"Magdalena?"

"My given name is Magdalena Carlota Erickson, now Erickson-O'Brien."

"Wow."

"My father is Swedish; Carlota was his mother. My mother is Spanish. They met in Spain, hence the Magdalena. No one other than my mother calls me that."

"Magdalena, for Mary Magdalene?"

"No." Maggie grinned, more relaxed now that the topic changed. "For *magdalenas*, the little Spanish muffins. My father claims my mother ate them incessantly while she was pregnant with me. He calls me Muffin, by the way, when he isn't calling me Buttercup."

"Do you have any brothers and sisters?"

"Four; I'm the next to youngest."

"Are you close to them?"

She thought about the question for a moment. "I'm really close to my older sister, Kim. My younger one, Jessie, irritates me pretty regularly, and my brothers are great—Carl is a doctor, Neil is the one who designed my security system—but I don't see them terribly often."

"And your parents?"

"Hold on a minute." She took him by the hand. "Come with me," she said, and led him down a darkened hall to a pine door. "This is my office."

Inside, Andre found himself in a room filled with bookshelves. A window seat overlooked a flower garden, and a computer sat on a desk piled with books, papers, and battered manila folders. One wall was finished with rustic panels of pine and covered with photos. Maggie pulled him toward the end of the pictures, next to a wooden spiral staircase. She pointed to a small picture of an older couple. A tall man with thinning red hair had his arm around a regal-looking dark-haired woman. Maggie's sons held onto her skirt, waving at the camera. "Those are my parents. They're alive and well in Arizona. Several times a year they come east and either stay here or in Montreal with Kim."

Andre studied the pictures in silence. Tucked to one side was a faded black and white photo of a bullfighter. Next to that was a picture of a tiny girl in a matador's jacket. "Who's that?"

"You can't tell?"

Andre looked closely and recognized the smile. "That's you?"

"That was my grandfather, Miguel Angel. He was a famous matador. My mother was his only child."

Andre gestured toward the staircase. "Where does that lead?"

"To my room. C'mon, I'll give you the ten-cent tour."

The staircase ended in the corner of a bedroom. Windows covered two sides of the room. Andre tried to set aside thoughts of sharing the wide bed with Maggie. "This used to be the carriage shed portion of the house. The previous owner remodeled it into rooms, but when I moved in, I added the staircase so I can work without disturbing the boys."

Down the hall, two toy-filled rooms shared a bathroom. "These are the boys' rooms." Maggie then opened a further door, "This is the guest room and there's a bath through there."

"Did your husband ever live here?"

Maggie corrected him automatically as they started down the central staircase. "My ex-husband. No, I bought the house when I got the job here and got my divorce settlement. When he's on leave though, he does stay here, in the guest room, so he can be with the boys."

"Does he stay here often?"

"Occasionally."

"How often is 'occasionally?'"

Maggie stretched her neck, trying to lessen the tension in her muscles, "Andre, let's go downstairs and make ourselves comfortable. We need to have *the* talk."

In the kitchen, Maggie poured them more coffee, and retrieved a box of gingerbread cookies, placing them on the table. They sat down again, and she twirled a spoon in her hands for a moment. "Okay, do you want to go first, or should I?"

Even agitated, Andre recognized how hard Maggie worked at being open with him. Perhaps he should return the favor. "I will."

"Were you sorry your marriage ended?"

He shook his head. "By the time we filed for divorce, I just wanted the whole thing to be over."

Maggie took a sip of coffee while debating how much to probe. "Tell me what happened."

Andre pondered. "Do you mean why we got married, or why we got divorced?"

"Both, I guess."

An hour later, after a lot of soul baring from both of them, Andre rose to use the bathroom, and when he came back to the kitchen, Maggie was massaging her temples. "What's wrong?"

She shrugged apologetically. "I have the beginning of a headache. I guess baring my soul made my head hurt."

Without thinking, he put his hands on her shoulders, slowly massaging her tight muscles. "I've put you through the wringer this morning, haven't I?"

Her response was quick. "No!" She shook her head and tried to soften her voice. "I mean, no, I want to do it if it'll help us work this out. I'll just duck upstairs and take an Advil."

Andre smiled and for a moment, Maggie felt hopeful in spite of her head. "How about you take an Advil and have a rest. Then I will take you to dinner tonight, and we can see where this goes?"

"You mean it? Like, you're not going to walk away without looking back?"

"No, I'm not. I'll pick you up at seven?"

Maggie's smile was blinding. "I'd love that."

Chapter Twenty-One

That evening, Maggie stood in the kitchen, obsessively checking her watch — at times, certain it stopped. Five minutes before Andre was due to arrive, she needed to sit down because her heart was racing. *Stop it! This is stupid. You've been on dates before. You've been on a date with **him** before!*

She stood up and hurried to the full-length mirror again, checking one more time to make sure she didn't have lipstick on her teeth. *Why are you acting like a blushing virgin? You passed that point with him already. Stop acting like such an idiot.*

The sound of a car door closing announced Andre's arrival. After a deep breath, Maggie walked to the front door, trying to appear completely relaxed.

Andre strode up the steps and smiled to see her through the screen door. "Hi."

"Hi."

He stepped over the threshold and gently touched her arm. "How are you? Does your head feel better?"

"Yes, thanks for asking. I took a quick nap this afternoon and it broke. Are you ready to go?" As the words left her mouth, the phone rang. Her face showed her inner struggle over whether to answer. *What if it was about the boys? What if it was Javi?*

"Deja vu," Andre nudged her arm. "Maggie, answer the phone. I'll wait."

Relieved to have the decision made for her, she hurried to the phone. "Hello?"

Javi's smooth voice flowed through the line. "Hola, Maggie. How are you?"

She should definitely have left without answering. "Good, and you?"

"Goodness, that's all you have to say? How was your concert last night? I'm sorry I missed it." His concern should have touched her, but instead his constant sweetness irritated the hell out of her.

"It was a wonderful concert, and the weather was perfect." Sweat began to form on the palms of her hands as she tried to think of a way to end the conversation.

"Am I interrupting something? You sound rushed."

"Oh, it's just that I was on my way out the door."

"You are? You didn't mention you had plans tonight?"

"Yes, I am."

"That's it for details?" Javi paused, waiting for her to say something, but when she didn't, he continued, "Well then, I'll let you go. I'm going to the final Zarzuela performance tonight so I should go too. How about breakfast tomorrow?"

Maggie bit her lip, unsure what to say. Should she say yes? She was essentially still dating him, so it would be a normal thing to do, but she wanted to be with Andre. Should she say no, out of her heartfelt hope he would still be here for breakfast? Damn, when did she ever need to *pick* between men? "I can't make it tomorrow, but I'll give you a call at some point."

His voice was a bit cool. Did he know? "Talk to you then."

Hanging up the phone, Andre stood silently, watching her. "Javi?" he ventured.

Maggie bristled, but before she could answer, he continued. "I notice you didn't say I was here."

Her answer was curt. "Andre, what do you want from me? A couple of nights ago, you were ready to hang me. Last night you all but spat on me when I got in your car, and now you're here, buying me dinner. Forgive me, but I don't have the foggiest fucking idea what is happening between us, and I didn't take any time today to call Javi and try to clarify things. Frankly, he's my least significant concern right now."

To her great surprise, Andre started to laugh. "Damn, Magdalena, fair enough, I apologize for sending mixed messages. Let's get some dinner and figure this out."

At the restaurant, they ordered quickly and settled into a quiet conversation of mostly safe small talk. Halfway through the meal, Andre stopped eating to look lingeringly at Maggie. "Maggie, I'm trying."

Maggie understood his meaning. "I know you are."

"More than anything, I want this to work. I'm still having problems. But I am trying."

After dinner, they drove back to Maggie's house in almost complete silence. Parked in the driveway, she said, "Do you want to come in? I mean for a nightcap, or a talk, or whatever."

Andre's grin was sexy, "Last time we "whatevered," we didn't stop until the next morning. Is that what you're suggesting?"

Maggie blushed. "Come in and we'll see."

Inside, Maggie snagged a bottle of merlot and two glasses and brought them out on the deck. Once she poured, she handed Andre a glass. "Here's the thing. I know what I feel. I'm so endlessly sorry I didn't let you know about the boys sooner, but I can't take that back. I can't make it better no matter how much I want to. Having said that, I'd give anything to go forward. You're here now and this is what we wanted in New York — to be together. I'd like to try, knowing full well you didn't, and probably don't, want children. I hope we can work it out. I can't spend every single moment on pins and needles, wondering if you've forgiven me, or if you're going to throw it in my face again."

Andre was silent and Maggie's heart sank. After a long pause, she asked nervously, "Do you have anything to add?"

"Yes."

"'Yes?' That's it?"

He rubbed his forehead, trying to find the right words. "Damn, Maggie, I see your face, hear your voice, and deep down, I know you did what seemed right to you at the time and now you regret it. So, I guess I'm on my way to forgiveness." He reached over to take her hand. "You have to understand this is a lot to adjust to at once." Lightly, he stroked the palm of her hand. "But one look at you, and it's all I can do to keep my hands off you."

Part of her rejoiced at his words, but she still heard the caution in his tone. "So, you're saying you're not sure if you'll completely forgive me, but you'd like to go to bed with me?"

"No, that's not what I'm saying! Well, yes, I'd *love* to go to bed with you again, but that's not *all* I'm saying."

Maggie tried to be understanding, but she had enough. "Andre, as for the physical part, sure, I'd love to go to bed with you again, but I'm not begging, and I'm not changing who I am."

Andre leaned toward her. "You don't need to change who you are or beg." His voice was almost a whisper as his lips were only millimeters from hers, "I'm the one begging. Please…"

Maggie felt herself melting as his lips touched hers. At first, the kiss felt sweet and gentle, but passion flared within seconds. Maggie gripped his shirt, needing more. Andre broke the kiss. "Please."

Without speaking, she stood up, pulling him by the hand. Moving quickly, she led him through the house to her room. The only light came from the almost-full moon shining through the gaps in the front curtains. She moved to sit on the edge of the bed as his finger moved to trace the valley between her breasts. "Andre, wait. I have to tell you something."

He kissed her neck, his tongue darting out in a tantalizing dance, "It can wait. This is more important than anything you have to say right now."

She tried to concentrate. "No, you need to listen to me," she implored.

Frustrated, he stopped. "What is so important that you want to stop?"

"I wanted to tell you you're the only man to use this bed with me. I mean, I bought it after my divorce, but you've been my only…"

Her words inflamed his passion. "Lover. I've been your only lover."

As he lay down beside her, slowly unzipping her dress, he stopped, needing to settle something before he made love to her. "Are you breaking up with Javi? Or am I going to listen to the two of you on the phone again tomorrow?"

Maggie threw herself back on the pillows, feeling dread temporarily consume her. She wanted to break it off with Javi, but more, she wanted to make love with Andre right then and there. "Seriously? You want me to break it off *now*?"

He rolled on his side, gently running his fingertips over her breasts, watching her nipples tighten. "Well, no, as long as we know where we stand."

"We know." Maggie rolled on her side and kissed him, desire filling her with warmth. The nagging voice in her head wouldn't stop. She rolled away, "Damn it, I have to do this now."

"That probably would be best."

She picked up the cordless phone, "Frig."

"Do you want me to leave?"

"No!" She turned to look at him, knowing if she reached Javi and Andre wasn't in the room, it would be hard to be firm about her decision. "No, please stay." She dialed Javi's number, praying he wouldn't answer. Five rings, six, seven, Maggie heard the message start. She prepared for the beep, then spoke in as calm of a voice as she could manage, "Javi, it's Maggie. Javi, I know this is a crappy thing to do by voicemail, but I was calling to talk to you because I need to break it off between us. It wouldn't be right for me to continue to let you think our relationship is growing when I'm not committed to it. I'm sorry for doing this over the phone and I really do wish you the best." She paused for a brief moment. "Good-bye Javi." She hung up and turned to look at Andre, who quickly tried to rid his face of his smug smile. "You enjoyed that, didn't you?"

He laughed, pulling her toward him possessively. "Yes, I did, I admit it. I wanted to kill him the other night for trying to make damn sure I knew you were with him, when I knew it wasn't over between us."

"Really?" Maggie leaned forward to plant a light kiss on his lips, "So now that I'm single again…"

"You're not single, you're with me!"

"Prove it."

Chapter Twenty-Two

The next morning, Maggie awoke abruptly from a sound sleep with Andre wrapped around her. What was that sound? Anxiety flooding her, she thought she heard footsteps on the porch. She sat up quickly, rousing Andre. "Someone's here."

"What?"

"Someone's on the porch."

Andre sensed the fear in her voice, "I'll go see who it is."

"No! My house, I'll check." Maggie stood up and looked out the window. "Fuck!"

"What is it?"

"Javi's here." Maggie grabbed jeans and a shirt out of the dresser, not bothering with anything else, hearing the first knock on the front door. "I'll be back."

"I'll go with you."

Maggie leaned down and kissed him briefly, "No, you won't. Stay here, please."

Andre's desire to protect her clashed with his desire to keep her stress-free. "Okay."

Maggie walked down the stairs, realizing she looked like she just rolled out of bed. She got to the door just as Javi raised his hand to knock. Plastering a smile on her face, she opened the heavy door, keeping the screen door closed and locked between them. "Javi. What are you doing here?"

"Good morning." He looked at her searchingly, clearly making note of her reddened lips and lack of a bra. "I think we need to talk."

Maggie sighed, "Javi, I don't think there is anything else to say. I said what I needed to say in my message."

His voice became sharper, "And I don't have the right to say anything in response?"

In her heart, she knew he was right. "Of course, you do."

"May I come in?"

Maggie hesitated, "I don't think that's a good idea."

"Maggie! I know Andre is here. I can see his car, so let me in. You owe me at least that much. I don't want to talk to you through a screen door."

For a month, Maggie hoped Javi would be more assertive in their relationship, and yet now, his sudden bossiness angered her. "Javi, we have nothing more to talk about, and you're not coming into my house. Either say it here or I want you to leave."

"Fine, if you won't let me in, I'll say it here. You let me believe you wanted to date. You let me believe we had a chance together. You lied!"

"Javi, I wasn't lying."

"Yes, you were. You clearly had something going on with Andre, and you used me in the process."

Maggie's voice was emphatic, "Javi, that isn't true. Yes, something happened between Andre and me in the past, but we both thought it was over. His coming here was a complete surprise to both of us. We didn't know we would meet again; you have to believe me. I would *never* have gone out with you if I thought Andre and I would get back together. Never."

"Again, I'll say you're lying."

The idea two men thought her a liar in such a short space of time was more than Maggie could stand, "You have the right to your opinion, but you'll have to leave now!"

"I'm not done!"

All of a sudden, a strong, warm hand settled on Maggie's lower back and Andre's voice cut through the air, "Yes, you are. Maggie asked you to leave, now you're leaving."

Javi looked at Andre with rage, "How dare you even enter into this conversation."

Later, Andre would apologize to Maggie for how he worded his response, "I'm the man who slept here last night, with Maggie. I'm the one who woke up next to her this morning. I'd say I have the right to be in this conversation." His hand still on Maggie's back, he gestured with his other hand, "Please go."

Javi looked at Maggie, "*Puta*! You wouldn't even allow anything more than a kiss, and barely that. Yet you slept with him right away!"

Maggie snapped, "*Puta*? You just called me a *puta*? Get the fuck off my property!"

After he drove away, his tires spraying gravel as he accelerated in anger, Andre looked down at Maggie. Without a word, she stalked to the kitchen, moving toward the sink. He followed her. "Maggie?"

"Not right now." Her hands shook as she filled the coffee pot with water.

Gently, he took the pot from her hands and turned her body around, wrapping his arms comfortingly around her. He was shocked when she started to cry quietly, her tears wetting his t-shirt. "Shh, Maggie, it's okay. Don't cry."

Andre's comforting remarks made her cry harder, and all he could do was hold her while she wept. Finally, as her breathing started to return to normal, she pulled back and looked up at him. "Thank you."

He brushed a lingering tear away, "What are the tears for?"

"He called me a puta, a whore. No one has ever called me that before."

"Baby, he called you that because he was mad; mad because he wants you and can't have you. He was striking out. You're *not* a puta."

Maggie looked seriously at him, "And you! You really thought announcing to him we slept together would help the situation? I told you to stay upstairs."

"Maggie, I heard the whole conversation. He told you he saw my car, he brought me into the conversation, and dammit, I won't let you be in *any* situation where someone could hurt you while I sit in a back room." He stroked her cheek, "I care about you. I have this incredible urge to protect you, and I couldn't just stay upstairs while he verbally attacked you."

"You care about me even though you're still mad at me?"

"I'm not mad at you anymore." He pulled her closer, bending over to kiss her. "And no one is going to bother you when I'm around."

Maggie wrapped her arms around his neck, kissing him deeply. Within seconds, desire consumed them, and Andre picked her up, never breaking the kiss, to carry her back to bed. As he stripped off his clothes, he watched her through darkened eyes, "I think you're overdressed…"

Maggie quickly shimmied out of her jeans and t-shirt, "What about now?"

"Perfect!"

Days later, Maggie called her sister. Kim's voice sounded irritated. "Where the hell have you been? I've sent you about nine million emails and left three messages. You couldn't take five minutes to call me?"

"No, I couldn't. I was too busy," Maggie's voice was smug, "With Andre."

"What?!? Tell me everything!"

"Well, we went to dinner last week and dinner led to drinks on my deck, which led to a kiss, which led to bed. Bed led to the hot tub, which led to bed, the couch, the car, and so on." She giggled.

"Holy shit. Oh, my God. Oh, my fucking God. I don't believe it."

"Yup, you can believe it. I'm just calling now because he's run home for a bit, and the boys are coming back later today, so he won't stay tonight, but he's going to have dinner tonight with me, Jake, and the boys."

"And he's okay with the boys?"

"*Okay* is a strong word. He's trying. I told Jake we're back together, and he's going to be on his best behavior. I guess we'll see how it goes."

Chapter Twenty-Three

That night, Maggie was unable to stay still as she made stuffed shells for dinner. She was so excited to see her boys again, and so nervous about Andre being there with the boys and Jake. What if Jake did something stupid? What if the boys were tired and obnoxious?

A little before five, she heard the car and ran to the front door. She was down the steps as Eli opened his car door. "Mommy! Mommy, Mommy, Mommy!"

Maggie picked him up in a hug, so happy to have his wiggling body home. "Eli! I missed you guys so much!"

Jake helped Nick out of his car seat and Nick ran around the car too. Soon Maggie was lying on the lawn with the two boys, laughing as they hugged each other and rolled around on the grass. She was so intent on her sons; she didn't hear Andre's car pull in. He got out of the car, walking over to stand next to Jake. Jake held out his hand and Andre shook it, "Andre. Good to see you again." He motioned to the threesome on the grass, "Sometimes I can't figure out who's the biggest kid, the boys, or Maggie."

Hearing her name, Maggie suddenly realized Andre was there. She jumped up, brushing grass off her clothes, straightening her shirt. "Andre! I didn't know you arrived," she said, and walked over to him. "Nick, Eli, do you remember Mommy and Uncle Devon's friend, Andre?"

Eli spoke first, "Yes, but Daddy says he's your boyfriend now."

Maggie looked at Jake in horror. "Jake!"

He shrugged, "Relax! We talked about it on the way here." He grinned, "I thought we should probably have an explanation for why Andre was here, and Javi wasn't."

Rolling her eyes, she walked toward the house, muttering, "You should have at least warned me that you told them..."

Dinner went well. The boys were on their best behavior, and Maggie was shocked at how well Jake and

Andre got along. At the end of the evening, Jake took the boys upstairs to get ready for bed, and Maggie walked Andre out to the car. She leaned up against the car and he put a hand on either side of her, looking at her searchingly. He smiled, "Thank you for a great dinner."

She smoothed the front of his shirt, "Thanks for coming."

"Maggie, I had a good time tonight." He paused, "Better than I expected."

"Me too. Thank you."

"So, if I'm your boyfriend, may I kiss you goodnight?"

She smiled, "Of course." She put a hand on the side of his face, "I'm going to miss you tonight. I've gotten used to you being here."

"I'm going to miss you too." He leaned down and kissed her gently. "See you tomorrow? Or at least talk to you tomorrow?"

"Perfect."

An hour later, Maggie and Jake sat down in the rocking chairs on the porch, each with a cold beer. Jake took a swig, then smiled at Maggie. "I like him."

"What?"

"Andre. I like him."

Her tone was sarcastic, "Well, I've been waiting for your approval…"

"Yeah, yeah, yeah. Seriously, Mags, he's a good guy, one who fits with you." He tipped his head, "You know, the boys weren't thrilled about Javi."

"What the hell are you talking about? They liked him!"

"Maggie, you dumped him, remember? You don't have to get all wound up protecting him now. Anyway, they tried to like him to make you happy, but Eli told me he didn't like Javi."

"Really?"

"Really. As for Andre, they don't know him yet, but when I tucked them in tonight, they commented they liked that he makes you smile a lot."

As much as Maggie didn't want to talk with Jake about her love life, it helped to hear this. "Thanks, Jake."

"You're welcome." His voice was really serious, "Mags, even though we're not together anymore, I still want you to be happy." His voice cracked, "I still love you, even though we aren't *in love* anymore. With Andre, I see the sparkle in your eyes again, the spark in you. It's been a long time since I've seen you that aware of anyone."

"You know this is a weird conversation, right?"

"Maggie, I loved you since I was sixteen years old. For many of those years, no matter how badly I hurt you, I was still *in love* with you. I've loved you for more than half my life. You are the mother of my children, and I want you to be happy; both for you and for them too. When you're happy, they're happy. When I hurt you and you were so sad, they felt it too, and I will always regret hurting any of you."

A rush of emotion filled Maggie, and she blinked back tears. "You know, sometimes you can be really sweet."

Chapter Twenty-Four

The next few days of Jake's visit passed in a blur. Maggie tried to squeeze in every possible private moment with Andre while also giving the boys the chance to spend as much time as possible with Jake. She was walking a tightrope, but the boys' smiles and Andre's ardent kisses made it all worthwhile.

When Jake left, the boys were devastated, and she finally had to talk to Andre about it. One night after the boys were asleep, she lay in the hammock on the deck with him. "I guess we have to cool it for a while; the boys need me right now."

"What do you mean?"

"They're so sad now that Jake's gone, and they really understand that he's deploying. I need to focus on them." She chuckled, "I should also try to focus on my job too for a bit, since classes start next week."

"I get the need to be with them and the need to get ready for the school year. I mean, I spent the day putting together my lectures for next week, but why can't we also make *us* a priority?"

"Because they need me more right now, and I have to make them the major priority."

Andre felt frustration building. "I need you too. Why can't we find a middle ground?" He kissed her gingerly, feeling her immediate response. Damn, but he was desperate to make love to her right now! "One where you feel the boys are getting what they need." He kissed her again, "And we're getting what we want, and need, too. Like right now I need to be inside you, feeling your heat, knowing there is no one between us during that time. I'm trying to be patient, but not making love to you for over a week is killing me."

Part of Maggie wanted to just shut up and go to bed with him, but her brain wouldn't stop. "Me too. But you know how I feel about this. I don't feel comfortable yet with the idea of you spending the night with the boys here." She tried to pick her words carefully, "Until we know this will last, I don't want them to get their hopes up that you'll be around forever."

He pulled back, "Are you saying you don't see this as 'lasting?'"

"No, Andre, I'm not saying that at all. What I am saying, is I don't know where you're at with the issue of the boys, and I need to know before I can go further with being physical with you when they're around."

"Damn, Maggie. I'm not just talking about the physical here." He touched her face gently, "I admit I'm about ready to chew through my steering wheel in sexual frustration. I get within half a mile of you and I'm ready. I hear your voice, smell your perfume, or even see your car, and I'm obsessed with the idea of making love to you. But it's more than that. I hate us calling each other so late to say goodnight when we could cuddle together. I want more than just a quick feel, and a 'see you later, sailor.'"

Maggie started to laugh, "Sailor?"

He sounded hurt, "You know what I mean."

"I didn't mean to hurt your feelings. I do know what you mean, but what about the boys?"

"I really like them, and I'm learning how to act around kids." He rested his hand on her hip, gently but possessively, "*This* is important to me, *you're* important to me."

Maggie grabbed his shirtfront to pull him close, "Fair enough. How about I see if the boys can stay with

Mike tomorrow night for a while so we can have a date? Maybe we could stay at your place for a few hours…."

His appreciative growl was all the answer she needed.

The next night, Andre stood in the kitchen of his apartment, putting the finishing touches on their dinner, when he heard a soft knock on the front door. "Door's open!"

Maggie entered, seeing him in the kitchen. He turned and took in the vision of her in a soft, flowing dark green dress accentuating her gorgeous curves and highlighting her long, slender neck. "Damn, you're beautiful."

"Thank you." Maggie came into the kitchen and stretched up to kiss his cheek. "Hi."

"Hi." Pulling her toward him, he kissed her with all of his pent-up desire, glad to finally not have an audience of little boys. Within seconds, his hands slipped down to her waist, pulling her even closer to him, his arousal very apparent. Her response was just as passionate.

Andre pulled back, "Sorry, it's been a long day, waiting to see you."

Maggie smiled at him, "Will anything be ruined if dinner waits?"

Andre looked at her, seeing the sparkle in her eyes, "Nothing will be ruined."

She giggled, "Well then, you know, I'm your landlord and should probably inspect your apartment to make sure you're following the lease."

"Oh really? What exactly are you looking for?"

"I was thinking I probably need to make sure you are taking care of the bedroom."

With a laugh, Andre scooped her up and threw her over his shoulder. "Really now, Madame Landlord, so I need to take you to my bedroom?"

"You do!"

The only light in the bedroom came through the French doors overlooking the creek. Andre placed her on the bed gently, and then quickly lay down beside her. "But you look so beautiful…"

"Are you saying you don't want to?"

"Oh, hell no!" He rolled over to brace himself with his forearms on either side of her. "I have you here with me, no one else around, and you're in my bed. I plan to make love to you." He kissed her neck, smiling as she arched her back to allow him easier access. "To remind you of what we have together. Then I'll feed you dinner and later, maybe sneak you back to bed for a bit."

Three hours later, Maggie stretched contentedly beside him, almost purring, "Damn, now *this* has been a date."

"Really?"

"Really." She kissed his bare shoulder, "Amazing lovemaking, a fabulous dinner, and you for dessert."

Chapter Twenty-Five

Over the next month, Maggie and Andre became adept at stealing a few hours together alone when they could, spending hours together with the boys, and balancing their work and private lives.

At the end of September, Andre called Maggie at work. She was at her desk when her phone buzzed softly beside her. "Hey."

"Hey, yourself. How's your day going?"

"Busy, but good. You?"

In his apartment, Andre leaned up against the kitchen counter, suddenly concerned she would turn down what he was proposing. "Good. Just office hours this morning. I'm home now."

"And you didn't bring me lunch?" she joked.

"I would have!"

"I know, I was just kidding. What's up?"

"I have an idea." He took a deep breath, "So, I'm being honored at an event two weeks from now in Boston, on a Saturday night. I didn't plan to go, but I was now wondering if we might be able to go together."

"Like for the weekend?"

"Or at least the Saturday night. We could drive down on Saturday, come back Sunday, stay at my place, go to the dinner…"

Maggie heard the tension in his voice. "I'd love to. Let me see if I can make arrangements for the boys and I'll let you know."

Fifteen minutes later, Andre's phone vibrated with a text. He smiled as he read it, *How about a Friday and Saturday night?*

He dialed her and smiled when she answered on the first ring. "Friday *and* Saturday? How did you manage that?"

"Kim says it's a Canadian holiday, so she'll come down Thursday night and stay until Sunday afternoon. We get two whole nights together."

Andre shifted uncomfortably as his immediate arousal pressed against his pants. "Two whole nights."

Just then, he heard background noise, "Sounds like you need to go."

"I do. I'll call you tonight?"

Andre forgot she had a school meeting that night. "Sounds good. I'll be up."

Two weeks later, Kim was just pulling a suitcase from her car when Andre arrived. Getting out of his car, he offered, "Let me help you with that."

She smiled, "You must be Andre."

"And you must be Kim, the saint who is making this weekend possible for us."

On the ride to Boston, Maggie and Andre chatted quietly, soft music playing on the stereo. They stopped for coffee in Holyoke, and as they walked back to the car holding hands, he grinned at her. "I think this is the first time I've seen you look completely relaxed."

She beamed, "I *am* relaxed, and it doesn't happen often."

They parked in front of his townhouse and got out of the car. They each pulled their bags out of the trunk and walked to the front door. In the foyer, Andre held out his hand. "I'll take your bag up to our room. Feel free to look around."

While he carried the bags upstairs to the bedroom, Maggie wandered through the main floor of the house, trying to tamp down her sudden discomfort at such a luxurious house. As she walked into the kitchen, she suddenly stopped, seeing a bouquet of red roses in a vase, with a bottle of champagne in an ice bucket, and two flutes next to it.

Just then, Andre approached from behind, wrapped his arms around her, and pulled her close so he could lean down to nibble on her earlobe. "Welcome home."

"Mmmm."

"I think those flowers are for you." He chuckled. "Remember the first time I sent you a rose?"

Maggie turned in his arms and reached up to unbutton the top button of his shirt, "I remember."

"What do you remember?"

The next button was undone, and Maggie felt her heart racing, "That you promised me dinner and a movie, and I never saw the movie."

His hands slipped up under her blouse, and with his fingertips, stroked her bare back with the lightest of touches. "As I remember, it was your idea to bag the movie and stay in." His voice was innocent, "But, I did promise you a movie, so if you want to go to a movie right now, we can go."

Maggie had unbuttoned two more buttons, "No, no movie. You, me, that champagne, and your bedroom, now."

He grabbed the ice bucket and glasses, "As you wish."

In his bedroom, Maggie paused, "I hate to say this, but I want a shower first."

His grin was wicked, "Sounds like a great idea."

In the bathroom, Andre shrugged out of his shirt, dropping it into a laundry hamper before dropping his jeans into the hamper as well. Clad only in his boxers, he strode over to the shower, turned on the water, then placed two fluffy towels on the small bench next to the shower. He turned toward Maggie. "Seems you're overdressed again."

She realized she was blushing. They made love before, and certainly, she was naked in front of him then, but undressing in a well-lit room suddenly seemed difficult. Taking a steadying breath, she grasped the hem of her blouse and pulled it up over her head, then slipped out of her slacks. Andre stood and watched, growing harder when he saw her lacy bra and panties.

He walked over to her, his eyes burning for her. "Here, let me help you." He crouched, hooking his fingers in the lace on one of her hips, and then slid the panties down her legs, his fingers trailing down her skin. Standing up again, he gently unhooked the bra clasp nestled between her breasts, then used both hands to push the rose silk down her arms until it, too, lay on the floor, the heel of his hands brushing against her breasts. Never taking his eyes from hers, he slipped off his boxers, then took her hand and led her to the shower. He checked the water, stepped inside, and pulled her in under the warm spray.

As he picked up a bar of soap, he stepped toward her, slowly lathering his hands then moving so he could wash her back. Coming back around, he lathered her front, stopping when she stood on her tiptoes to kiss him, her wet body pressing against his. He picked her up, her legs wrapping around him, "Damn, I want you. Here, now."

"Me too."

He slid into her, slowly made love to her, feeling her body respond. Long moments passed filled with words of endearment, then conversation stopped when passion overcame them.

Later, dressed in bathrobes, they sat on the loveseat in the alcove off his bedroom. He opened the bottle of champagne, then handed her a small envelope. "This was in your flowers."

Maggie opened the envelope and pulled out a small card. The note was brief: *Thank you for moving mountains to be here with me this weekend. Yours, Andre*

Maggie turned on the couch to stroke his cheek, "You're welcome. Tell me, how could you be in Vermont with me yesterday, but have all this set up here today?"

He shrugged, "My cleaning lady treats me like her son. I never brought a woman here like this, so she was thrilled to be my partner in crime."

"Please thank her for me."

The rest of the weekend passed in a sexy, luxurious blur. Friday night, they finally dressed and went out for dinner overlooking the harbor, before coming back to the house to make love by candlelight. Saturday morning, they slept late, went out to breakfast, then took a walk through the Commons before dressing in formal wear for the dinner.

Andre was dressed, working on his tie, when Maggie came out of the bathroom. Her black dress wrapped around her curves like a second skin, and physical arousal hit him like a wave. He walked toward her, admiring every inch of her beauty, "Magdalena, you are absolutely stunning."

"Thank you." Her look was shy, "I don't think I've ever worn a dress that left this little to the imagination."

He ran a finger down the side of her neck and then traced the lacy edge of the dress as it dipped between her breasts. "You look simply spectacular, my love. Every man there will be trying to get your attention."

She reached up to straighten his tie. "They're out of luck then, because you're the only one I care about."

At the party, Maggie was introduced to one person after another, and tried as hard as possible to keep names and roles straight. Andre kept a protective and possessive arm around her, and even when they weren't physically touching each other, he was never far away.

After the dinner, Maggie watched with pride as Andre was recognized for his work in pro bono employment cases. As he accepted his award, his gaze was warm as he looked at Maggie, "And to Maggie, thank you for being here tonight with me. I can't tell you how much it means to have you in my life."

Chapter Twenty-Six

Two weeks later, Andre was just unlocking his front door when the phone in his pocket buzzed. It was Devon.

"Hey, Dev."

"Andre."

His tone was off. "What's wrong?"

"I need your help."

"Of course, what?"

"I'm headed to the college to get Maggie. You heard what happened when she was in Mississippi?"

Dread filled Andre instantly. "Yeah."

"Her brother just called me. He got word from his sources that Joel Nadeau is being granted a parole hearing. He's petitioning he's no longer insane, so he should be allowed to stay in a mental hospital, but not one with the security he has now."

"Are you fucking kidding me?" Andre took a deep breath, knowing he needed to think like a lawyer, not like Maggie's lover. "What do you need from me?"

"If it's okay with you, I want to get her and bring her to your place where the three of us can talk without the boys around. Her brother is working on getting more details for me, but I'd like your eyes on this too to make sure I'm not missing anything." He took a deep breath and Andre heard the stress in his voice, "Like you, this is personal for me. I want to make sure we don't fuck it up. I figure we'll only get one shot to make sure he can't ever get near her again."

"I'm home. Bring all the files you got on the case. I'll see you in a few minutes."

Ten minutes later, Andre heard a car door slam. As Devon and Maggie walked through the door, he noticed the telltale signs of anger in her flushed cheeks, but it wasn't until the door closed behind her that she exploded. She turned to Devon. "You! You had no right to pull me out of the office to do this! No right at all. And you had *less* right to involve Andre in this!"

Devon stood calmly, "Can I say something?"

"No! You had no right! I can handle this. And my brother, damn him, he had no right to call you first." She pulled her phone out of her pocket, trying to swipe to get to the contacts, but her hands shook so badly, she needed several attempts. Devon and Andre just stood and watched her, knowing she needed to do this. "Neil. You asshole! You had no right to call Devon first. You should have called *me*." They heard a male voice respond until Maggie cut him off, "I don't *care* that I'm your baby sister, I'm still an adult, and you had no right to treat me like this. You should have called *me* first, then let *me* decide if I wanted to involve anyone. I swear to God, Neil, I'm telling Mom you did this!" Whatever her brother said, Andre suddenly saw a smile form on Maggie's face, "Yes, I did just yell at you for not treating me like an adult, and in the same sentence I threatened to tell Mom on you." She laughed. "Fuck you, too."

Maggie stood by the windows, looking out at the falls, listening to her brother intently. Finally, she pinched the bridge of her nose, a headache beginning to form. "I know you're just protecting me, and I love you for it, but you're still an unbearable, over-protective pain in the ass." She turned to look at Devon and Andre, "Yeah, they're both here and Dev has the whole file in the back of his car, so I assume they're going to do the lawyer thing. I'll call you later. Love you."

Maggie hung up, looked at the two men in silence. Finally, in a resigned voice she said, "Fine. Do your lawyer thing."

Devon looked at her, "Okay, I'll get the files."

With Devon gone, Andre walked toward Maggie, noticing her ashen skin, save for the splotches of red remaining from her waning anger. He extended his hands. "Hi. You okay?"

Maggie took his hands, offering a strained smile. "Fine. I'm *fine*."

"Really?" He pulled her toward him, his hands now resting on her upper arms. "Really?"

Maggie looked up, her eyes filling with tears. He pulled her close and wrapped his arms around her tightly, feeling her shake like a leaf. "It's okay, Maggie, I'm here."

"It's *not* okay. If it isn't now, it'll be next time. He's going to get out, and neither I nor the boys will ever truly be safe again, never."

He kissed her hair, "We'll figure this out. I promise, you'll all be safe."

Devon returned with the files and placed the hefty box on the table. Maggie looked at the box, then looked at the two men seriously. Her voice trembled, "I can't do this. Forgive me, but I need to go back to work and let the two of you read this all over. Talk to Neil or whatever you need to do."

Devon shook his head, "No, Mags, we need your input on this."

Andre raised a hand, seeing Maggie's stress level increasing. "Dev, how about you and I go through the files here this afternoon, and I can get up to speed? Maggie can return to work, then come back here in a few hours when I'm better prepared. In the meantime, I assume Neil will be getting us more details and we can form a plan." He put his arm around Maggie, "Okay?"

Maggie forced a smile. "Okay. That sounds good."

Andre kissed her temple. "Take my car back to work and then plan to come back around three thirty. The three of us can talk, and I can take you and the boys out to dinner tonight."

Maggie knew how hard Andre was trying to make her feel more settled. "Okay," she said, then picked up her purse, walked around to hug Devon convulsively, "Thanks, Dev. Thanks for always having my back."

"Always, Mags, always. Just like you have mine."

Andre walked Maggie out to his car, handing her the keys, "You okay to drive?"

She nodded, "Yeah." Leaning against the car, she held both of his hands, "Do you understand why I need to go back to work right now?"

"Because you need to feel safe, in control. Sitting here watching us roll around in the mud would just make it worse."

"Exactly. By the time I get back, I'll be ready to do whatever you both feel I need to do, but right now, I need to do what makes me feel like I'm in control of my universe." She stood on her tiptoes and kissed him briefly. "Thanks for understanding. Thanks for helping me with this." She pulled back and Andre saw a blush creep up her cheeks, "Andre, I know how much you get per hour for your legal advice. I need you to bill me for this."

He leaned down to rest his forehead against hers, "Not happening, Magdalena. Not a chance." He stroked her cheek, wanting nothing more than to sweep her into his arms and take her upstairs to help her forget the horrors of her past. "You're part of my life now, and I'm not billing you for advice on keeping you safe."

Immediately, he saw her tense, ready to argue with him. "But that's not right!"

"It is right." As the wind blew, a piece of hair fell across one of her eyes and Andre gently tucked it back. "Do you care about me?"

"Of course, I do."

"Then that is all I need as payment." He kissed her briefly. "Now, go back to work, and I'll see you in a few hours with a battle plan."

Two hours later, Andre looked up from the last pile of papers and gazed at Devon in horror. "Holy shit, this is worse than I thought."

"Yeah, I know." Devon sipped his now cold coffee, grimacing. "Obviously, you see I wasn't representing Mags in the proceedings. I was just there as support. Her lawyer, Ted Limoges did a great job. Nadeau is certifiably insane, and yet, there's a damn good chance he'll win and get moved to a minimum-security facility."

Flipping back through the file, Andre's tone was clipped. "Were you there for the whole trial?"

"Every minute."

"And the notes about the evidence, was it as clear as it sounds?"

"Andre, they had life-sized pictures of what he did in her apartment. Posters of his journal entries, posters of what he did to his own mother after she told him he couldn't marry Maggie. Even being a prosecutor in New York, I've never seen anything like this. Trouble is, as I see it, Nadeau had only the one major incident where he *committed* violence and was convicted of it. The rest is *just*—not to make light of it, but—the rest is *just* his fantasies of violence against Maggie. And after how badly the psychiatrist in Mississippi missed the warning signs, I don't have much faith this group is any better at determining whether he's a threat to her."

Just then, Devon's phone rang. "Hello? Neil, good, I'm here with Andre and he's reviewed the files." Devon put the phone down on the table and turned on the speakerphone. "Neil, can you hear us?"

"Yes. Andre, sorry we haven't met in person."

"Likewise."

"Thanks so much for what you're doing with all of this."

"No problem."

Neil chuckled, "So, Devon has probably told you, I could be considered a slightly over-protective brother, but it's good to have you involved. Great work on the Haskins case."

With his comment, Andre realized Neil clearly ran a background check on him, at least a professional one. Interesting… "Thanks."

"Okay, so here's what I know. Nadeau will go before the parole board two weeks from today. Normally, we wouldn't know it, but you both know I have the case tagged so I get notifications on any changes. Because he didn't actually *hurt* Maggie, she doesn't get the automatic notification. He isn't asking to be released, as in *freed*, he's asking to be moved from the maximum-security psychiatric prison to a minimum-security psychiatric hospital. He's claiming he realizes he needs to stay hospitalized but is asking to be moved from the locked facility."

Andre leaned back in his chair, "What are the security precautions at the proposed facility?"

"Guards at the door. Bed checks at night. Supposed med checks during the day. Five-foot fence around the property."

"Does the fence have sensors?"

"No."

"No ankle bracelets? What about sensors on the windows?"

"No and no."

Devon sat back, watching Andre's expression with interest. Andre made notes on a legal pad, "Does Nadeau's mother have any living relatives other than him?"

"Yes. A brother."

"And what is he thinking?"

"He wants him locked up where he is. He feels he's a danger to society."

"What are the psychiatrists saying?"

"That he's compliant, takes his meds faithfully, and hasn't had a violent incident since his first year in lock-up."

"What happened then?"

Neil sighed, "Maggie doesn't know this, and I'd prefer it stay that way ..."

Andre's heart sunk, "Shit, that doesn't sound good."

"You'll keep it quiet?"

"Okay."

"Thanks. It would just hurt her to know this." Neil paused. "In his first year, an orderly noticed Nadeau kept a private journal separate from his required treatment journal. He was taking pages out of the required one and hiding them under his mattress. The pages were all about how he loved Maggie and his fantasies about what would happen when he got out. Talk of how they'd be married, the same old shit. From what they pieced together, he would write about her every night after lights' out, then masturbate while thinking of her. When all this came out, his journal was confiscated, and they told him they would search his room regularly. The next night, he beat the orderly so badly, he was in the hospital for weeks."

"And Maggie doesn't know this?"

Neil shook his head. "She was pregnant with Eli. Nadeau was locked up, we knew he couldn't get to her, and everyone already knew her marriage with Jake was rocky. Devon and I talked with Jake and decided she didn't need to know."

Andre rubbed his forehead. "Shit. I certainly understand why you did it, but the trouble is, the best argument we have for keeping him locked up is what he did to the orderly. Either we can't use that, or she needs to be told."

Devon nodded, "Neil, I agree with Andre. Maggie needs to know."

There was a long silence. "She will be livid we didn't tell her, and she's already living with the guilt of his mother's death. This will make it worse."

Andre leaned back in his chair. "I agree, but Neil, without this information, he will be released. I know we don't want to hurt her more emotionally, but this may be the only way we can keep her safe."

Devon and Andre stared at each other, waiting for Neil's response. He growled. "You are right. Christ, I hate this, but we do need to tell her."

Over the next ten minutes, the men decided how to proceed. They agreed Neil would contact Kim about coming down for the weekend, Neil would fly up from Washington, and they would work together to plan for Neil and Devon to attend the hearing and testify. Just as they were about to end the conversation, Andre heard footsteps on his outside stairs. "Maggie's here."

Devon and Andre heard Neil exhale sharply, "Shit. I hoped we'd be done before she got back."

Andre's voice was sure, "She has to know *now*. It's not fair for all of us to know, waiting for you to get here before we tell her."

Neil snapped. "Fine. Let her in and I'll tell her."

Andre went to the door and opened it. Maggie was about to knock, and Andre noticed with concern her pale face. "Hi."

She offered a stressed smile. "Hi."

He pulled her into a hug, "How was your afternoon?"

"Okay. Yours?"

"Better now that you're here." He kissed her, immediately feeling her relax into his arms, as if seeking comfort. "Come in."

Andre pulled her toward the table and Maggie noticed the phone. She shook her head, "Lemme guess. Hi, Neil." She ventured.

"Hey, Mags."

Putting her purse down on the couch, she continued, "The fact you're on the phone must mean you're going to tell me something I'm not gonna like, right?"

"No, yes." Neil cleared his throat. "I've been texting Kim. She's coming down for the weekend and I'm flying up. Kim will help with the boys while you and I, Devon, and Andre plan how Devon and I will testify at the hearing."

"Okay." From Maggie's tone, Andre knew she was braced for more. She sat down, her head resting on one hand. "Just say it, Neil. Whatever it is, just tell me."

Neil calmly told her about Nadeau's first year of incarceration. Maggie listened in silence until he finished. "Mags, you still there?"

"I'm here."

"Say something."

Her tone was curt, "There's nothing to say. You should've told me, but I know you did what you thought was best at the time." She sat up straight as Andre and Devon watched her morph back into her professional persona. "Neil, I reviewed the Mississippi guidelines this afternoon. If he's applying to be released to a less restrictive facility, his psychiatric records have to be included in the proceedings. Can you get a copy?"

"I would think so, why?"

She picked up a pencil and pulled a pad of paper over. "Because this is *my* area of expertise. Get me the files. All of them. I need to see them, even if you think they'll upset me. If you can get them to me before the weekend, I'll have time to look for holes so we can maybe find something of use."

"Done. I'll start the request paperwork right now."

Over the next ten minutes, the group made plans for the weekend. At the end of the conversation, Maggie picked up the phone, turning the speaker off. "Okay, Neil, that's it for today. We'll talk tomorrow?"

"Promise. Love you."

"Love you, too."

After hanging up, Maggie handed Devon the phone. "Thanks, Dev, for everything."

He hugged her close, "You got it." He looked back and forth between Andre and Maggie, "Hey Mags, how about I go pick up the boys and take them home for a bit? Give you guys a little time alone? I can grab your car at the college and leave mine there. I'll tell them you're picking up grinders for dinner and will bring them to the house when they're ready."

The idea of a few minutes alone with Andre was so appealing, Maggie jumped at the idea. "That would be awesome. Why don't you pick up Claire too, and we can all have dinner together?"

"Great."

Once the door closed behind Devon, Andre looked at Maggie. "Come here."

Maggie slowly walked toward him in her bare feet. Andre held out his arms and she hugged him tightly, the top of her head barely coming to his shoulder. Her words were muffled by his shirt, "Thank you."

"For what?"

"For spending the afternoon trying to protect me."

"Anytime."

Chapter Twenty-Seven

That Friday evening, Andre realized he was following a car as he turned into Maggie's road, then both vehicles turned into her driveway. As the vehicle stopped in front of her house, Andre figured it was probably her brother, Neil.

Andre got out of his car and approached the visitor. A tall, blond man, with eyes eerily similar to Maggie's, got out of the car, looking at Andre intently. "Andre, I assume?"

"You assume correctly." Andre held out his hand, "Andre Serapes."

"Neil Erickson." His handshake was firm. "Nice to meet you."

"You, too."

Neil stopped, his voice serious, "Thank you so much for your help and support."

"I won't say it's been a pleasure, but I'd do anything for Maggie."

Over the weekend, the group brainstormed how Devon, Neil, and Andre would present Maggie's case to the parole board, while Kim and Mike amused the boys. Much of the weekend, Maggie just listened, saying almost nothing.

Sunday afternoon, as the group of adults sat on the deck drinking beers, Maggie suddenly whispered, "I'm going."

Kim was sitting between Neil and Maggie, "Where?"

"To Mississippi."

Neil spoke before Andre had a chance. "Bullshit. You are staying here. We've got this."

Maggie looked at her brother, her face calm, and her voice even. "No, I'm going. This is not up for discussion. This is *my* life. I'm going, I need to actually see what happens, and the board needs to see *my* face to make it personal." She looked down at her hands, knotted in her lap, "I've already talked to Mike. He'll take a few days off this week to take care of the boys. Because of work, I'll fly down the day after you guys and meet you there."

Andre's stomach clenched at the idea of her facing Joel. Before he could argue with her, Devon broke in, "I have to agree with Maggie, as much as I prefer keeping her here, I think she's right."

Kim nodded, "Me too." She reached over to squeeze Maggie's hand, "Do you want me here to help Mike, or do you want me to go down to Mississippi?"

Maggie felt her heart swell with love for the group in front of her, "Here. Help with the boys, please."

"You got it."

Neil sighed, "Fine. You are an irritating, stubborn pain in the ass, you know that, right?"

She smiled. "Of course I am, big brother. After all, I'm related to you aren't I?"

Two hours later, Maggie came back into the kitchen after saying goodbye to her brother and sister, Devon and Claire. Andre was loading the dishwasher, and Maggie heard the familiar sounds of a Disney movie from the living room.

Andre pulled Maggie by the hand, leading her outside to one of the rocking chairs. Sitting down, he pulled her down to sit on his lap. He smiled as she laid her head on his shoulder. Beginning to rock, he kept his voice gentle. "You could have mentioned going to Mississippi before this afternoon."

"I know." Her voice was small. "I knew if I brought it up before then, you'd all argue with me." She ran her fingers up and down the trim on his shirt. "You aren't mad, are you?"

He kissed her hair. "Maggie, I'm not mad at all. Worried and concerned? Yes. Mad? No." He kept rocking. "I would prefer to keep you as far away from this bastard as possible, but when I consider what I would tell a client, not my lover, I would say the board needs to see your face, to see how this is personal."

"Thank you."

"So, you'll fly down on Thursday?"

"Yeah, you guys go down on Wednesday, get ready, I'll arrive the following day, then I'll come back on Saturday."

"We're staying until Monday, since the board won't announce their decision until then."

"I know. Kim can't stay that long, and I don't want to be away from the boys any more than necessary."

"Okay." His arms tightened around her, "Any chance I can share a hotel room with you while we're there?"

Maggie tipped her head back, pulling his head down to hers, kissing him deeply. Heat swamped Maggie as she realized how much she wanted him. As Maggie pulled back, she lightly rubbed her thumb across his lower lip, "That's the *real* reason I'm going to Mississippi…"

Chapter Twenty-Eight

Entering the concourse of the airport four days later, Maggie's heart jumped when she saw Andre waiting for her. As he took her carry-on, he leaned down, nuzzling her cheek for a second before he kissed her. "Hi. How was your flight?"

"Fine."

"Ready to go to the hotel?

Maggie smirked, "Can't wait to get me naked?"

He laughed, his arm possessively around her, "Well, yes, but I thought we could go back, get you settled, eat, do a quick review, *then* I could get you naked."

The next morning, Maggie was curled contentedly next to Andre. He rolled over, his hand warm and comforting on her bare hip. "Good morning."

She purred, "Good morning," she said with a smile, and continued to stretch. "You know, considering what we have going on today, I shouldn't feel this good right now."

"Once this is over, sweetheart, then we can make sure you always feel this good in the morning."

Two hours later, the group's car pulled up to the gatehouse of the prison. Neil was driving, and he opened the window to show the guard his pass. Inside the main building, all four of them went through the metal detectors, then were escorted to a conference room. Two couples sat outside the door. When the younger man saw Maggie, his face paled, and he stood. "You're Maggie, aren't you?"

Maggie felt her nerves tingle at the thought of a stranger knowing who she was in this setting. "Yes, and you are?"

"Octavio Ruiz, ma'am."

Maggie's stomach dropped, having finally read all of the details of Joel Nadeau's attack on this man.

"Octavio," she said as she stepped forward and the two of them hugged. Her eyes swam with tears, "I'm so sorry you got hurt because of me. I am so, so sorry."

He looked surprised, "You didn't hurt me, that animal did."

"That is kind of you to say, but indirectly, it was because of me."

"No, ma'am. He owns this, pure and simple."

Over the next few minutes, Maggie was introduced to Nadeau's uncle and his wife, as well as Octavio's spouse. Andre watched with interest as Maggie became more and more comfortable with them, realizing she wasn't alone in her fears, and seeing they didn't blame her for the hurt inflicted upon them.

At the appointed hour, a bailiff came to the door and called for interested parties to the proceedings. Octavio and his wife, Nadeau's uncle and his wife walked into the room first, then Devon and Neil, and finally, Maggie and Andre.

Maggie was seated behind Octavio. As Nadeau entered the room, he clearly didn't see her there. The head of the parole board called the proceedings to order, and then Nadeau's lawyer presented his petition and stated the rationale for the move. In a clear and concise manner, the lawyer assured the committee Joel Nadeau had been a model prisoner since his move to that facility, and all indications were that he would continue to follow all rules and expectations in a less restrictive institution.

The head of the board then asked if any members of the audience wanted to speak to the petition. Nadeau's uncle spoke in a halting voice about going to the house with the police and finding his only sister brutally murdered. In a wavering voice, he begged the board to deny the request to release his nephew to a facility with less security.

When Octavio rose to speak, Nadeau saw Maggie for the first time in years.

Though he was shackled, he stood up, yelling, "Maggie! Maggie, you came! I knew you would, honey, I knew it!" The guards tried to restrain him, pushing him back down into his chair, but he wouldn't be seated. "Maggie, I love you honey! I'm doing this for you, baby. For you! At my new place, you can come see me every week. We can be together!"

The guards finally wrestled him back down. The chair of the board looked at him with disdain, "Mr. Nadeau, you understand this is a hearing to make a decision on your petition to be reassigned to a less restrictive environment? You are grossly ignoring the rules of this proceeding." He shook his head, "From this point forward, Mr. Nadeau, you are not to speak, and you are not to address members of the audience. Your lawyer will speak for you. Do you understand?"

"Yes, sir," his eyes never leaving Maggie.

Octavio then spoke on finding the secret journal, talked about what was in the journal, and how Nadeau attacked him the next night. He spoke of lying in the hospital for weeks, the lingering pain in the shattered knee, and how his life had changed.

When Octavio finished, he sat down, reaching back to squeeze Maggie's hand. Devon and Neil then spoke to the board about their concerns for Maggie's safety if Joel were removed from a maximum-security facility. When they finished, the chair of the board looked to Maggie directly. "Mrs. O'Brien, do you have anything to add?

Nadeau yelled, "Don't call her that! She's not *Mrs.* O'Brien!"

The chair ignored him, "Mrs. O'Brien, anything to add?"

Maggie was taken aback, feeling completely off-guard. Andre leaned close and put his arm around her protectively. "You don't need to add anything, Maggie."

"Yes, I do," she said, and stood, squeezed his shoulder, and walked calmly to the now-empty chair. Looking at the chair of the board, she swallowed. "I ask you to keep Mr. Nadeau as originally sentenced, here, in a maximum-security facility, for the duration of his sentence. You saw here today he still has delusions, believing we're a couple; he still thinks we'll be together, and if he's in a less secure facility, I feel he would be a risk for flight and would put me, the other witnesses here, as well as the larger community, at risk of harm. Please."

Nadeau implored the board chair, "I'm not a risk for flight, I promise. I'll stay in the hospital, just let me go there where I can live a real life, please. Please. I'll do exactly what I'm told, I promise!"

Maggie walked back toward Andre, keeping her eyes locked on his. He stood when she came back to him, and she stood on tiptoe to kiss him. As her lips touched his, Nadeau erupted in the chair, "Don't you dare touch her! Don't touch her!"

"Mr. Nadeau, you have been warned!"

Nadeau ignored him, screaming. "Don't you touch her, you son-of-a-bitch. I'll kill you for touching my Maggie. I'll kill you!"

Guards swarmed forward, eventually removing a screaming and kicking Nadeau from the room.

The members of the board sat stunned. The chair then addressed the public. "Obviously, this proceeding did not go exactly as we anticipated. As required by law, the board will meet this afternoon to discuss the petition, and will deliver its ruling to the warden, Monday morning, at nine a.m." His words sounded perfunctory. "If you disagree with the ruling, you will have twenty-four hours to appeal."

Maggie was silent as they left the prison. She got into the car without a word and without looking at any of the three men. With Devon behind the wheel, Andre sat in the back seat with Maggie. He reached over to take her hand, squeezing it gently, trying to get her back with them.

They were about two miles away from the prison when Neil pulled down the visor mirror so he could see his sister. "Mags?"

Her voice was quiet, "Yes?"

"Forgive the question, but did you kiss Andre because you just wanted to kiss him, or because you knew what would happen?"

Maggie looked out the window for what seemed like a long time, to a point where Neil wasn't sure she heard the question. Turning to look at Neil, a sparkle returned to her eyes. "I kissed Andre because I kinda like kissing him," she said, and blushed, "but yes, I also knew it would set Nadeau off."

Devon looked at her in the rearview mirror, "How'd you know that?"

She grinned, her natural color returning to her face, "That's why I wanted his records. The night he attacked

Octavio, he kept telling him he'd kill any other man who touched me."

The rest of the trip was a quiet, conversational debriefing. At the hotel, Maggie looked at the three of them, and smiled. "Gentlemen, I want lunch. I want Mexican food with a big-ass margarita or two, then I want a pedicure."

Neil laughed and gave his sister a gentle shove. "Two margaritas? Shit, after this morning, I think we should have them bring bottles of straight tequila. But otherwise, that sounds like a plan!"

The next morning, Andre walked Maggie up to the security checkpoint at the airport. Putting her bag down, he pulled her close. "I wish you weren't going home today."

"Me too."

"Or... I wish we were going together."

"Me too."

He stroked her cheek, smiling as he saw her eyes darken with desire, "I'm going to be lonely tonight, sleeping in that big bed all by myself."

She noticed his look immediately soften as it caressed her. "I don't remember sleeping a whole lot over the last two nights."

He chuckled, "Point taken," he said, and kissed the tip of her nose. "Go home, call me whenever you want, and I'll see you Monday night."

"Dinner at my house?"

"Perfect."

Monday morning, at exactly 9:01, Maggie's phone rang as she sat at her desk at work, nervously waiting. "Yes?"

Andre's voice was jubilant, "Petition denied!"

Maggie let out her breath in a whoosh, suddenly light-headed with relief, "Really?"

"Really. Denied."

Neil grabbed the phone out of Andre's hand, "Mags, it's done! It's done!"

That night, Devon, Claire, Andre, Maggie, and the boys barbecued on the deck, laughing, and celebrating.

After Devon and Claire left, Andre pulled Maggie out to the back deck, leading her to the hammock. Once she was snuggled against him, he slowly stroked her back, his voice sure, "Now we can get on with our lives. You're safe."

"I'm *safe*."

Chapter Twenty-Nine

Over the next month, Maggie often wondered if she was living a dream, or beginning a nightmare. Each night, as she lay in bed waiting to fall asleep after talking on the phone with Andre to say good night, she thought about the day. She had to admit Andre made every effort to show how much he wanted to be in her life. He was with her many nights out of the week for dinner, took them to movies, and even attended soccer games. She saw he consciously thought about how he treated the boys, and how he treated her when they were around. When they were apart, he would call and ask about their days, but she admitted it still felt forced. When they were by themselves, their relationship was absolute perfection. When the boys were around, Maggie felt like she was on a tightrope, trying to be a good mother and lover.

One night everything came to an unexpected boiling point. Andre came to dinner and seemed more relaxed than normal with the boys. After eating, he helped rinse the dishes. "So, how was work?"

She shrugged. "Busy. I need to return some calls when we're done. It was so busy; I couldn't get them done at the office."

He strode to where Maggie was preparing lunches for the next day, noticing her tense posture. Taking the clementines from her hands, he pulled her toward him. She put her arms around him, leaning against his chest, enjoying as she always did, the feeling of touching him, breathing in his scent. He kissed the top of her head, "I'll finish up here; you go make your calls."

"Really? What about the boys?"

"Really. Go do what you need to do, and I'll keep them busy while you work." He kissed her again quickly, "Hey guys, come help me with your lunches and then we'll play."

Eli and Nick came running into the kitchen, visibly excited to help Andre. Maggie smiled and stretched up to kiss his cheek, "Thanks."

Working in her office, Maggie heard the sounds of laughter in the living room and for a moment, began to believe it might really work.

After putting the boys to bed, Maggie came downstairs to find Andre on the couch, looking at his lecture notes for the next day. Standing behind him, she kissed the back of his neck. "Mmm, you smell so good."

Andre motioned toward the cushion next to him. "Come, sit down and make my day."

Within minutes, the two of them were stretched out, kissing fervently. When Maggie pulled back, she lovingly touched his face. "Thank you for keeping the guys company while I worked. They were so excited upstairs talking about playing Legos with you."

"You're welcome. We had fun."

He kissed her again, but she wanted to continue the conversation. "Were they being good?"

"Very good."

"And you didn't mind?"

"Maggie, I didn't mind. They were being so good. And so was I."

Maggie was beginning to be distracted by his kisses. "You were what?"

"Being good." His hands slid up under her shirt, his caresses becoming hypnotic as they came closer and closer to her breasts. "I was being good, too. Now don't you think my being good deserves some," he lightly licked the side of her neck, "adult time?"

He might as well have thrown a bucket of cold water on her. Later, she would wonder if she overreacted, but at that moment, all she heard was the bargaining tone. She sat up so quickly she almost fell off the couch. "You played Legos in order to have sex?"

"No! I just meant that, you know, I've been really paying attention to helping out, so you'd be happy."

"So, this isn't about you actually being okay with all of this? It's about you putting on an act for me!"

"No, Maggie, dammit, it's not an act. I was just trying to say I am trying to be more aware how I can support you, make you happy."

"Oh, my fucking God, you've been playing along like things were better, hoping I wouldn't know it was an act, and we'd still…" Maggie was so angry, she couldn't finish the sentence. She sat with her mouth wide open, staring in disbelief, then stood. "Get the hell out, Andre. You accused me of not telling you the truth in New York and yet you've been playing a game all this time."

"What game?"

"That you like the boys. That you're okay with me having kids. That we had a chance as a couple."

"I *do* like the boys, and we *do* have a chance."

"Not if you're play-acting all the time." She wrapped her arms around herself tightly, "And to play mind games about my boys? That, I won't fucking forgive. Get the hell out!"

"Are you serious? Maggie, I was just saying it would be nice to have some 'us time,' that's all."

"Bullshit, you were saying you offered to hang out with them tonight to make me happy, so I'd make you happy."

"I did want to make you happy, still do. What's wrong with that?"

"What's wrong with that is you spent time with my children so you could get laid." She pointed toward the door, "Get out. Now."

"You're being ridiculous, and you know it."

"Get the fuck out!"

"I will not! You need to be reasonable here."

Later, Andre would realize using the word *reasonable* was like waving a cape in front of one of her grandfather's bulls.

Her eyes glittered dangerously, "Get out now or I'll trigger the alarm system and have the police haul your ass out of here."

"Fine. I'll leave now, but we're going to talk about this when you calm down. We've come too far to give up now."

"Get out!" Maggie yelled, not caring who heard her at that point.

Chapter Thirty

Maggie was pouring coffee into her travel mug the next morning when her phone buzzed with a text. From the ringtone, she knew it was Andre. *Can we talk?*

Maggie thought about ignoring the message but knew he would push the issue. *No.*

Why not?

Because I'm not ready to talk.

When do you think you'll be ready?

When I am.

Seriously, that's your answer? Doesn't this mean more to you than that?

Really pissed right now, not ready. She paused, then sent one more, *Leaving for work in a few minutes. Will try to be ready to talk this afternoon.*

Do you want me to come over?

No. Phone or text. Not ready for in-person.

Why?

Because if I see you, I'll forget why I'm mad.

If you can forget that easily, is this really a big deal?

Don't push it.

Okay. Call or text me.

Later that afternoon, Maggie drove into her driveway with the boys chattering in the back seat. As they were getting out of the car, Eli asked, "Mommy, is Andre coming for dinner tonight?"

"No, buddy, just us tonight."

"But, Mommy, why? We like it when Andre comes!"

"Because sometimes Mommy likes to be alone with you guys for dinner."

Eli didn't hear the frustration in her voice, "But Mommy, we don't *want* to have dinner with just you, we want Andre to be here too!"

Maggie would later regret the way she spoke to Eli. "Eli, stop it! Andre isn't coming to dinner, he may not come to dinner again for a while, if ever, and I don't want to hear another word about it." She yanked her bag out of the car. "Now go inside and watch television while I make some calls."

Eli wasn't accustomed to her speaking to them like that. "Okay, Mommy. C'mon Nick."

In her office, Maggie tried to calm her emotions. Clearly, Eli and Nick really liked Andre, just as Jake said, and the only way she could continue to be with him was if he was really committed to the idea of being a family with the three of them, not just a visitor. She put her head in her hands as she realized either he needed to be able to commit, or they needed to end it, there was no middle ground. The boys' dad already moved out, and they couldn't deal with another loss in their young lives.

Slowly, she pulled out her cell phone, placing it on the desk. How could she deliver an ultimatum by telling him there was no middle ground anymore?

She hit speed dial, and Andre answered on the first ring. His deep voice made her heart ache, "Hi."

"Hi."

"How was your day?"

"Long. Yours?"

"Long. All I could think about was you."

"Me too."

"So, where are we?"

Maggie started to cry, struggling to keep her voice calm so he wouldn't know, "Andre, here's the thing: I know how I feel about you. If it was just me, we wouldn't be having this conversation, but the boys are getting attached to you, and I can't keep going unless you're ready to commit to it all."

"What are you saying? That we have to get married?"

"No! Just that I can't keep having you in my life—in *their* lives—if you still really don't want kids. You have to want it all."

"Jesus, Maggie, you can't just expect me to go from being single to having a family this fast!"

"I know that! But it has to be more than *trying*." Her voice broke and Andre realized she was crying, "Tonight Eli wanted to know if you were coming to dinner and when I told him no, he gave me a hard time. They already consider you a part of our family. I can't do that to them if you're not really invested in that part. They've already been through divorce. They already adapted to Jake living away from them, and I can't put them through another situation where they lose someone they love."

"Maggie, you know how I feel about you!"

"I do. But this isn't about what you feel for me. It's about what you feel for them."

"Maggie, I like your boys, I like being around them."

"But are you ready to be a full-time parent figure? If I get sick next week and can't take them to soccer, are you going to do it because you care about them, or because you think it'll make me happy?"

"Why can't it be because I want to make you happy *and* that I care about them? Why can't we let the rest keep growing?"

"Because we *can't*. I already had to spend nights with Eli crying because Jake wasn't going to move home with us. I can't do it again." As she stopped and sniffed, Andre realized she was wiping her nose. "Here's the thing, Andre. If you can't even say you're ready for this after we had a fight and seemingly broke up, then I know how you feel. So, it's over." She swallowed, "I've got to go. Goodbye, Andre."

"Maggie, wait!"

"There's nothing left to wait for. Goodbye." And she hung up.

Chapter Thirty-One

Over the next month, Maggie tried to stay upbeat, only letting the hurt and sadness show in her journal,

Two weeks, three days since we broke up. I can't believe it's really over. The boys are being absolute twits, whining day after day about when they get to see Andre again. I feel like all I do is bitch at them, but I can't take explaining it anymore. I keep telling them it just didn't work out. I miss him so much. I miss everything about him, as lame as that sounds. I kept hoping he'd reconsider and come back, but clearly, he really didn't want to be with us all and it was just a game.

Two weeks later, the phone rang. "How are things?" Kim queried.

Maggie's voice was barely audible. "Surviving. Just surviving. I spend all day running around at work, barely keeping up. I guess I should thank fuckhead Anderson for changing the program – I'm so swamped with the waves of student teachers, I don't have time to think during the day."

"And at night?"

"I come home, race around trying to give the boys time, do the house stuff, watch a bit of television, and fall asleep. Then I get up in the morning and start again."

"Have you seen him?"

Maggie didn't need to ask who Kim was talking about. "Yeah, he was at Devon's post-Thanksgiving party. We avoided each other like the plague."

"And he hasn't tried to call you? Or see you?"

"No. Not since the first two days. Luckily, he moves out in two weeks, and I assume he's going back to Boston."

"Damn, Mags, I really thought he was the one for you. I'm so sorry. Maybe you should have stayed with Javi."

Maggie shook her head. "No, Javi was never right for me, not really." Her voice dropped to a whisper. "I should have just stayed away from them both, period."

Chapter Thirty-Two

Six months later.

Maggie was half-heartedly dusting the bookshelves when she looked out the living room window as the car turned into the driveway. Her heart almost stopped when she spotted the four-door black sedan. In her entire life, such a car never brought good news to anyone. Where were the boys? Oh, thank God, they were over at Mike's playing with his new puppy.

Two men exited the car in military dress uniforms. Maggie's breakfast moved in her stomach as she wiped her hands. Walking to the front door, she opened it as one of them raised a fist to knock and immediately recognized one of the men. "Tom…"

Second Lieutenant Tom Chambers, Jake's best friend since basic training, stepped over the threshold, removing his hat. "Hi, Maggie. This is Captain Barilla."

Maggie shook hands with the second man in a daze, then gave Tom a hug, terrified of what came next.

His hat in his hands, Tom spoke quietly. "Maggie, I think we should sit down."

Her mother's lectures on politeness seeped bone deep. "Certainly. We can sit in the living room. Can I get you something to drink?"

Tom took Maggie by the elbow. "Maggie, come sit. We're fine."

In the living room, Maggie perched on the edge of a chair, the two men across from her on the couch. With sad eyes, Tom looked at Maggie, "You know why we're here."

She nodded, having trouble breathing. "Probably."

Captain Barilla spoke, his voice deep and smooth like a radio announcer. "It's with our deepest regrets we have to inform you of yesterday's death of Major Jacob O'Brien."

Maggie's first reaction was a burst of pure uncontrollable anger. "Yesterday? He died yesterday and you're letting me know now? My boys sent him an email last night and now I have to tell them he didn't get it because he was dead?"

Tom jumped up to move across the room and kneel in front of her. His hands were strong on her arms. "Listen to me, Maggie. Jake asked me to tell you if something ever happened to him. You know that. We picked each other back in the academy. I was on a training mission in Alaska and it took me time to get here."

"How?"

Tom understood her simple question. "His jet was hit by a surface-to-air missile."

Maggie remembered something. "The boys emailed him last night after they heard on the news a plane was hit. They were so happy it wasn't him." Covering her mouth, Maggie needed to swallow several times before the nausea passed, white spots dancing along the sides of her field of vision. "They panicked, but I kept telling them Daddy was fine." Reality was beginning to set in. "And he wasn't. That was him. It's only been in the last few weeks I watched the news with them because I was afraid of something like this." She looked at Tom beseechingly, "It was really him?"

Tom nodded. "Yes. They had the video going on his wingman's plane. They caught it all on tape. We hoped you didn't hear about it on the news yet..."

Maggie's thoughts swam with everything she needed to do. "I have to call my parents and make arrangements. And I need to tell the boys." Her voice cracked. "What the hell do I tell my boys?"

Captain Barilla spoke quietly, "You tell them their daddy died a hero and he loved them very much. Both are true."

The next week flew past in a blur. Maggie functioned in a daze, doing what needed to be done, and trying to be there for the boys every moment. They slept in her bed; afraid she would leave them too. The whole time, her heart ached with unshed tears.

Three days following the funeral, Maggie sat at her desk, sorting the bills from the funeral home, when she heard a car door slam. Where were the boys? The local paper kept sending a reporter, hoping for an article about how the family was falling apart. Maggie tiredly recalled the boys were with her parents at their hotel, packing.

Opening the front door, Maggie found Tom standing again on the top step, holding a cardboard box. "Hi, Mags."

"Tom."

"Can I come in?"

"Sure." In the kitchen, Maggie gestured toward the coffee pot. It seemed each day she needed more and more coffee just to function. "Would you like some?"

"That'd be great. Can I sit down?"

Maggie smiled and gestured toward a chair as she poured coffee. Carrying the two mugs and cream on a tray, she joined him at the table.

After a sip, Tom played with the spoon. "Maggie, Jake's belongings arrived today. They sent them to me to deliver."

This surprised Maggie. "I thought we already got everything. The base sent us a box last week."

"No, these were the things he had with him on duty that day, in his locker. They just arrived here. You and the boys should have them." He pulled the box onto the table. "Do you want me to take the stuff out?"

"No. I'll do it later."

An hour later, Tom left, giving Maggie a hug. "I'm so sorry, Mags. I know Jake screwed up in your marriage, but, in his way, he loved you. And you know he loved the boys more than anything in the world. Just remember that and help *them* to remember it."

Maggie carried the box onto the deck, placed it on the picnic table, and opened it. The first thing she saw was his extra flight suit. She set that aside carefully, knowing the boys would want to see it when the wounds weren't so fresh. A Clive Cussler novel was tucked to the side of the box, near a few CDs. That made her smile. Jake had held onto the older technology doggedly. Then, under a pile of clean white t-shirts, she saw it — his leather jacket.

Pulling it out of the box, she inhaled its familiar scent. Jake bought the jacket before they were married and it carried years of cologne, airports, bases, the boys, and him. The leather was battered and scarred, but in the collar, she still smelled traces of her perfume. Without thinking, she slipped it on, remembering how Jake slipped it over her shoulders the night they became engaged. She also wore it home from the hospital when Eli was born, because none of her jackets fit her. The ache in her heart was almost unbearable as she felt its familiar weight.

She heard paper crinkling in the pocket. Upon further inspection, she pulled out an envelope and a laminated picture of her, with Jake and the boys, at the ocean the summer before. Biting her lower lip, she slid a fingernail under the flap of the envelope and pulled out a letter.

Dear Maggie,

As hokey as this sounds, if you're reading this, I'm gone. Damn, if nothing else, I hope I went out big, not in some sissy way. (Did you at least smile when you read that?)

First, I want you to know that as I write this, I'm at peace. Every morning since Eli and Nick were born, I've been at peace because I knew they were with you – and there is nowhere I'd rather have them be. You have raised them to be incredible boys, who will someday be incredible men. And I thank you for that. I know how badly I hurt you, but you not only raised them without making them think badly of me – you helped them to admire me. I've never in my life felt prouder than when my sons told me this summer, they wanted to be just like me when they grow up. I know you'll continue to raise them well, with love and laughter and courage. Don't let them be afraid to live – please.

And I'm sorry. I guess I never really told you how sorry I was for hurting you. I loved you with all my heart and I guess I wasn't really ready to be a married man. I'm sorry for hurting you so badly.

Goodbye, Maggie O'Brien – I loved you and love you still. I will miss seeing you and hearing your voice, but I will still be there in spirit, keeping you company and laughing with you. Love our boys with every ounce of your being, for both of us, and never let them hide from life, love, or duty.

Love, Jake

The phone startled Maggie as she still sat at the table and read the letter over and over. "Hello," she croaked.

"Maggie?"

She felt as though she was swimming in molasses. "Andre?"

"Maggie, I just came home from Ireland and found a message from Devon, telling me what happened. I'm so sorry about Jake. How are you? How are the boys?"

"We're okay. Thanks for asking."

"Is there anything I can do?" He cleared his throat. "I mean it, Maggie, anything."

For just a moment, Maggie wanted to say, *come home, hold me, let me cry, take some of this weight off me*. Then she remembered how it ended. "We're fine. Thank you."

Andre heard the dismissal in her tone but felt compelled to continue. "Okay. And are the boys really okay?"

"Like you care. Goodbye, Andre." Maggie hung up.

Finally, the tears came, and Maggie cried as though she'd never stop.

Chapter Thirty-Three

Two months later, Maggie realized she made a huge mistake. When she saw the boys' flight connections, it made sense to just drive down to Boston and spend the night in a hotel before sending them on their flight to Arizona. That way, she'd see them off and have a short break alone before flying to London. In the months since Jake's death, she didn't have a moment alone. It was only in the last week or so that the boys agreed to sleep in their own rooms.

At first, everything seemed to go well in Boston. Eli and Nick looked so cute waving goodbye in the airport, holding hands with the young stewardess yesterday. But once they were gone, Boston grew cold and dull instantaneously. Even the skyline last night seemed colorless.

Maggie stood and looked out the hotel window, trying to maintain her meditation breathing pattern, finding it almost impossible to stay focused on inhaling and exhaling. Her suitcase sat on the bed behind her, neatly packed, and she had seven hours to kill until her flight to London. Who the hell was she kidding? Boston wasn't the problem, *she* was.

She was stuck alone in a hotel, afraid to go out because she might run into Andre. The thought that he might be out there turned her stomach. She could hold on to her resolve not to contact him, not to beg him to try again, as long as she didn't see his face or hear his voice. She even went so far as to archive pictures of him so she couldn't readily look at them on her phone.

Hanging around alone in a hotel room was stupid; she knew that. Moping was pointless. In a city as large as Boston, it was almost statistically impossible to run into Andre. So why not get out of the room, go for a walk through Quincy Market, and pick up a new book to read on the flight?

In Faneuil Hall, Maggie looked over several racks of magazines and books. Finally, she paid for two glossy magazines and a thick paperback. As she took the bag from the clerk, her stomach growled loudly.

Maggie blushed, but the young man behind the counter laughed. "Sounds like you're ready for lunch."

"Yeah. I guess I am."

"Well, like the man sang, 'you can get anything you want at Alice's Restaurant.'"

Maggie chuckled, amused to find an Arlo Guthrie fan. "Exceptin' Alice."

"Cool, most people don't get that reference."

In a better mood, Maggie walked through the spring air to the front steps of the Market, realizing how hungry she was. Slowly, she walked down the aisle, turning her head to make sure she saw every possible option. Normally, she would eat something disgustingly healthy, like a big salad, before flying. *Gag.* Salad as a meal was a tiny step above eating grass. Taking a huge breath, she held an internal negotiation – she'd eat a salad but treat herself to an ice cream after.

When her tray was loaded, she gingerly made her way to a corner table in the relatively quiet main hall. For a few minutes, she watched the other diners raptly as she munched. Her stomach rolled over unhappily, as she spotted a familiar dark head across the room, seated across from a stunningly beautiful woman. What the hell was Andre doing at Quincy Market? What the hell were the odds he would be there when she was? As she watched, the woman smiled at the man with a clearly seductive smile, laughing and tossing her head back, her perfectly cut hair swinging back like a shampoo model. For a moment, Maggie felt absolutely frumpy in her simple travel outfit until she saw the woman stroke his hand with her long fingernails, causing white hot anger to shoot through Maggie. *Who the fuck is this woman touching Andre?*

As Maggie continued to watch in disbelief, it began to sink in; shit, Andre specifically said he never visited Quincy Market, finding the hordes of tourists to be too much to bear. So why was he here today, of all days? Didn't she convince herself there was *no* way she'd see him? Did God think this was funny? Hadn't she endured enough cosmic shit lately?

Thinking blasphemous thoughts, she swallowed a huge bite without chewing, immediately coughing. A piece of carrot lodged firmly in her windpipe. She tried as hard as she could to free it, all the time praying Andre wouldn't notice the commotion. She turned away to avoid drawing attention.

Across the room, Andre caught a glimpse of reddish-blond hair swinging away. His heart stopped for a moment, and he forced himself to take a deep breath, sure there was no way it was Maggie. After all, what were the odds Maggie would be in Boston at Quincy Market? He shook his head, trying to clear thoughts of her, knowing he needed to focus on Lexi. He swallowed, internally chastising himself for his lack of enthusiasm about this burgeoning relationship. He needed to forget Maggie once and for all and focus on his future. Before turning back to his companion, he couldn't help himself and took one final longing look, realizing it was indeed Maggie.

Uncertain, he wanted to cross the room, but the memory of their last conversation burned in his mind. As he watched, Maggie stopped coughing and turned for a sip of water. As she drank, their eyes met, and her cheeks burned a bright red. Then Maggie coldly and clearly looked from him to the woman sitting next to him.

Her look was so icy; Andre felt the chill seep into his bones. She obviously didn't miss the tone of his lunch with Alexis.

Andre turned to Alexis, who was completely absorbed in her salad. Her long dark nails contrasted with the white plastic of the fork. Trying to forget Maggie, Andre took a long sip of his iced coffee. "How's your salad?"

Wiping her mouth carefully, Alexis smiled and brushed her shiny, smooth dark hair back off her shoulders. "It's perfect. Thanks." She reached out to squeeze his hand. "Thank you for coming to meet me for lunch. What a nice surprise." Her voice lowered to a sexy purr. "How about I return the favor by making you dinner at my place tonight?"

Damn! This should have been what he wanted. A beautiful woman who shared his career interests and love of the city was inviting him over. And she already made sure he understood she wasn't looking for complications. All he could think about was the very pissed-off woman across the room.

Even though he couldn't turn around without being obvious, the way his skin tingled told him she was still in the room and glaring. Fuck her, she could glare all she wanted, they were through as a couple. *She* made sure of that! His future might include Alexis, so Maggie could just sit and stew. After all, Maggie dumped him, then jumped down his throat on the phone.

Alexis wouldn't do that; she understood his goals, his interests, and his priorities. She even enjoyed reading the Law Review with him. While he didn't feel that absolute rush of passion when he saw Lexi, like he did from the very beginning with Maggie, maybe it would come with time. For all he cared, Maggie could sit across the room and fume. Her anger didn't matter to him; he could ignore her for as long as she was in the room.

Right, like he could *ever* ignore Maggie. Andre's mouth quirked as he pictured her sitting across the room making a voodoo doll out of carrots.

Making an effort to sound normal, he squeezed Alexis' hand back. "That sounds great. When I get back to the office, let me check the schedule and I'll call to let you know what time I'll be done."

"Great."

Andre took a careful bite of his sandwich, chewing slowly. Picking his words carefully, he feigned relaxation. "Lexi, I need to run across the room for just a moment to speak to a former ... client. It'll just take a minute or two."

Confident of her appeal, Alexis wasn't worried. "That's fine. I'll just call the office to see if Jeanette has finished typing the motion I need to file this afternoon."

Taking a deep breath, Andre gritted his teeth and stood. Turning toward Maggie, he walked across the room, feeling her ire wash over him. By the time he reached her little table, he was primed for battle. "May I sit?"

Her tone was cutting. "Why? You seem to have a perfectly acceptable table across the room."

His voice held a warning. "Maggie! May I sit down?"

She shrugged, then hissed in a cold voice. "Suit yourself."

As Andre sat on the wooden stool, he examined Maggie's face. If not for the telltale streaks of color on her cheeks, he might think his arrival didn't bother her. "Hi."

The one simple word pissed her off beyond all comprehension. "Hi? *Hi?* What the hell do you want, Andre?"

"To say hello."

"Done. Anything else? If not, leave."

"Well, it seemed like you weren't going to say hello to me, so …"

Her tone was sickeningly sweet. "Why, golly gee, Andre. Me and my poor manners. I didn't race right over to say hello to you and Ms. Perky Tits over there. What a social faux pas! I appreciate you coming over to illuminate proper behavior for me." She spat the last sentence at him.

Her biting sarcasm and comment about Lexi infuriated him. "Her name is Alexis!"

"Thanks for sharing."

Andre steadied himself, trying to regain control of the conversation. "What are you doing here? In Boston, I mean."

Maggie knew deep down she was acting like a bitch, but somehow her mouth seemed to be running with little filter. "I didn't realize I needed a reason to be in Boston. Did we divide up the country into regions? You know, Boston is your territory, Vermont mine, and we need to get travel visas to cross the borders?"

"I didn't mean it in a hostile way! I'm just wondering why you're here."

"Why are *you* here? You swore you stayed away from Quincy Market, that there were too many tourists."

Andre tried to think of a logical answer, but he was still too angry. "I came here for lunch. It wouldn't have been my first choice of places, but it's near..." His voice trailed off.

Understanding hit Maggie hard. "You mean it's near," her voice tightened, "Alexis. You figured it was worth eating lunch here in hopes you could get some."

The answer rushed out of his mouth. "I don't need to *hope* to get some. Lexi's a sure thing."

As the words entered Maggie's mind, Andre saw the blood drain from her face, her mouth agape, and her eyes reflecting how deeply his words pierced her.

Even through his haze of rage, Andre immediately wished he could take those words back. Maybe Lexi was a sure thing, but hadn't he just sat there trying to figure out what to do about her? Wondering why it didn't feel right? "Oh, shit, Maggie. I—"

"Wow." Her haunted eyes gazed sadly at him. She stood and gathered her garbage before picking up her purse. "Well, then. I don't want to keep you from a sure thing. They don't come along all that often." She stretched a bit to toss the cup in the trashcan, pleased when it went right in. "To answer your earlier question, I'm in Boston because the boys flew out of here last night to visit my parents. I'm flying to London tonight. I've been offered a job there for second semester, so I'm going to look things over, and if I like it, find a place for us to live."

As her words sunk in, a sense of urgency filled him, "What? Wait a minute. Maggie, we need to talk about this."

Her brow furrowed as she looked at him in confusion, "Talk about what, Andre? We broke up, remember? And you seem to have moved on just fine, so there's absolutely no reason for me to discuss my life choices with you."

How could he make her understand? "You know I care about you."

Her anger rushed back, "You fucking *care*? You just told me you have a 'sure thing' over there, Andre. I guess I was pretty easy to get over."

"Maggie, it's not like that, really."

"Andre, you're in a place you specifically told me you avoid, eating a meal with a woman who's flashing you 'fuck me eyes' and stroking your hand. You're *clearly* over me," she struggled to keep her voice calm, "which is fine. But then you somehow seem to think that you have the right to know my life plans." She shook her head. "Believe me, you gave up any rights regarding *me* months ago."

His shock was clear, "Are you saying you haven't been out with anyone since me? It's been *eight* months."

Her tone was scathing, "Gosh, Andre, you know, trying to put my kids' lives back together after grief almost destroyed them, on top of trying to settle my ex-husband's estate, while still working full-time, hasn't given me a lot of free time." Her eyes grew sad, "So, no, I haven't been out with anyone. But, again, that's not your business."

"Maggie, we need to talk about London."

She shouldered her purse. "No, we don't. Goodbye, Andre." With that, she turned and walked away.

Chapter Thirty-Four

Hours later, Maggie stirred restlessly in the airport lounge. If only they would call her flight. Couldn't they just hurry up so she could get the hell out of Boston?

When they finally called her flight number, she stood up and smoothed her black skirt. With her carry-on and laptop tucked under one arm, she waited impatiently in the boarding line.

Maggie stepped onto the plane, relief flowing through her as she walked down the aisle. Moving toward the coach section, she looked for her seat, then her heart sank. Damn! An older man was already there, meaning she'd have to ask him to move. All she wanted was to sink into her seat and get on her way. Instead, now she needed to interact with a stranger.

A flight attendant saw her looking at her ticket and the at the man. "May I help you?"

Maggie gestured. "That's my seat."

The attendant looked at the ticket, glanced at the man, and looked back at the ticket. Finally, she smiled seeing Maggie's name. "Oh, I'm sorry, Ms. O'Brien. I thought they would have stopped you at the gate. Your seat has been moved."

"What? I mean, I'm sorry, today has been the day from hell and I just want my seat. I didn't ask for a new seat; I want this one. Please."

The woman's voice was calm and gentle, as if talking with a cranky child. "Your seat has been moved to first-class. If you'll come with me, I'll help you get settled."

Maggie's head swam in confusion. "What? I booked a coach seat. One right here. Near the bulkhead. Near the bathroom. I just want to sit down. I don't want to pay for a first-class seat." Her tone became even more brittle as the ramifications of the change hit her. "I *won't* pay for a first-class seat!"

The attendant took Maggie by the elbow. "Ms. O'Brien, my understanding is that your seat was upgraded. You aren't paying any more for the seat, but you now have a better one. How about we get you settled, hmm?"

Maggie's nerves hummed in confusion. "Are you sure I'm not paying any more?"

Carefully, the attendant took Maggie's laptop bag. "Positive. Now c'mon, and we'll find your seat and get you something to drink. Perhaps a cup of tea?"

Completely overwhelmed, Maggie followed her toward the front of the plane. Her seat was on the aisle, with an empty window seat next to her.

Sitting down, Maggie sank into the soft leather. It cradled her tired body as the attendant handed her a cup of steaming tea. Maggie tried to be pleasant. "Thank you. I apologize if I seemed rude. Thank you for being so nice." For some reason, Maggie's eyes filled with tears.

The attendant snagged a nearby box of tissues. "It must have been an awful day for you. Don't worry about a thing, sit back, and relax. My name is Monica. Let me know if I can help in any way."

"Thank you, Monica." Maggie sat back to sip her tea, closing her eyes. Quiet bustling around her let her know other passengers were getting organized, but no one showed up for the window seat.

Finally, the pilot spoke into the loudspeaker. "Ladies and gentlemen, welcome aboard. We will be pulling back from the gate in less than five minutes. Attendants, please prepare for take-off."

Maggie tightened her seatbelt, feeling the sickening swell of nervousness as the engines began to rumble. No matter how many times she flew, take-offs and landings always made her nervous. She was so involved in her pre-flight prayers of negotiation with God, she didn't realize a man was standing next to her, ready to take the window seat. When he softly cleared his throat, Maggie looked up into Andre's dark brown eyes.

Maggie went from prayers to curses in less than a second. "*You*!?!? What the hell are *you* doing here?"

Andre's voice was perfectly calm. "I'm flying to London." He smiled, "What are you doing here?"

The urge to hit him was almost overwhelming. "I'm going to London, as you damn well know!"

"Well, I'm going *too*. I decided I need a vacation and today is as good a day as any." Andre's thoughts temporarily went to recalling everything he went through that afternoon to pull this impromptu trip together. "Now, if you'll excuse me, I'm booked for that window seat."

Suddenly it was clear. Maggie's first reaction seeing Andre was to think this was all a coincidence, but she understood with his last comment. "*You*! You changed my seat, so I'd have to sit next to you. How dare you!"

His tone became dangerously quiet, and Maggie realized how much emotion he was holding in at that moment. "How dare *I*? *You* drop a potential move to London as an afterthought to a conversation. Then you pulled an attitude with me. So, yes, I changed your seat. I called Mike and he had all the flight information. Kim helped me convince the airline this would be a wonderful surprise, and they booked us together into these seats. I paid for your seat, so don't yell about that."

"I can't sit next to you! I can't." Maggie frantically looked around for the attendant. "Monica! Monica!"

Monica appeared almost instantly. "Yes, Ms. O'Brien?"

"I can't sit next to this man. I need to move. I'll take any open seat."

"There are no open seats, we're completely full. What seems to be the problem?"

Andre smiled and shrugged. "Ma'am, I mean *Monica*. Ms. O'Brien and I had a quarrel, and I just wanted to try and patch things up between us, so I booked myself onto this flight." He patted the arm of Maggie's seat. "I guess she's not quite ready to forgive me."

Monica melted. "Oh, that's so sweet! Now that explains why she told me she had such an awful day. As soon as we take off, let me get you two a bottle of champagne, I'm sure that'll help things."

Chapter Thirty-Five

As the engines rumbled in earnest, Maggie worried less about Andre, and more about surviving take-off. She'd be damned if she'd throw up from nervousness in front of him. She still had *some* pride, after all.

Praying for serenity, she closed her eyes, unaware how shallow her breathing had become. Suddenly, a warm hand covered hers.

Her eyes flew open in surprise. "What the hell are you doing? Take your hand off me."

Andre's voice was soothing. "You can be mad at me after take-off, but you're about two seconds away from hyperventilating. Why didn't you tell me you're afraid of flying?"

"I'm not afraid of *flying*. I'm just fucking terrified of take-offs and landings. In between, I'm just fine."

Her sense of logic amused Andre and he chuckled. "Okay, I'll explain later why that makes absolutely no sense, but for right now, hold my hand. You can be angry at me and call me names again when we're in the air."

Maggie wanted to be so calm that she could refuse his offer of support, but damn, it would help a lot to hold onto him. "You won't hold my hand when we're in the air? You won't touch me?"

"I promise, unless you ask me to."

Maggie took his hand and squeezed it tightly. As the plane rose into the air, Andre wondered if his hand would break.

In the air, Maggie relaxed her hold. In a sullen voice, she muttered, "Thank you."

Andre's gaze was piercing, "Why didn't you tell me?"

"Tell you what?"

"How afraid you are of taking off."

"What are you talking about?"

"Mississippi, Maggie, I'm talking about Mississippi." His face was clearly pained, "How could you have suffered through flying down and back alone, so afraid, when one of us could have gone with you? *I could have gone with you.*"

Maggie looked down at her hands, "I couldn't tell you."

"Why? We were lovers, why couldn't you tell me that?"

"Because—" Maggie closed her eyes, her cheeks burning with embarrassment, "I made such a big deal of being strong enough to go down to Mississippi, I couldn't admit I was scared of anything. I just had to suck it up."

Andre stroked her cheek, his mouth tightening when she pulled away from his touch. "I hate that you were afraid, and alone."

She shook her head, "It doesn't matter now; it's done." She reclined her seat, her arms wrapped tightly around her, keeping as much distance as possible between her and Andre. "Thank you for holding my hand just now, it helped."

"You're welcome. Are you speaking to me now?"

"No. I mean, I don't know." She looked at him, clearly confused, "What the hell are you doing here, really?"

Andre took a deep breath before speaking. "I told you. I decided a trip to London was just the break I needed. I admit, I wasn't planning it, but after our conversation today, it seemed to be the right thing to do."

"'The right thing to do?' Andre, you can't just up and take off to London, changing my flight plans on a whim. Real people don't do shit like this. We broke up. It's over. You can't suddenly act like we're still a couple."

"Can't I? I did it. Call me romantic, but I thought it was a grand gesture. And tell me: are you really so pissed off at me that you're up here in first class rather than sitting back there in the cattle car?"

Maggie ran her hand over the leather seat. "No. I have to admit it will be really hard to go sit back there, but you had no right to do this. I made my plans, and you weren't part of them."

"I know, and that's my point; I *should* have been part of them. Not that long ago, we were part of each other's lives. Then it all fell apart, except at least for me, the emotion didn't end. So here I am now. And we are going to London *together*." He braced himself for her reaction to his next comment. "I changed your hotel reservation too. You're staying in a suite with me in a hotel across the street from Harrod's. But before you go ballistic, it has two bedrooms, so you don't have to stay *with* me."

Maggie's blood pressure rocketed. "You had the fucking nerve to change my reservation? How dare you think I would want to stay with you in London? I'm going to look at a job – not to be with *you*. You had absolutely no right to do this."

Just at that moment, Monica arrived with champagne. "Here you go; this should help everyone's mood."

Andre smiled at her, thankful for the break in the tension. "Thank you, Monica. Hopefully it'll help."

After the attendant moved away, Andre put his glass down and took Maggie's hand. He held onto it tightly when she tried to pull away. "Listen to me, Magdalena. I have something to say, and you're damn well going to listen to me. Afterwards, if you still want me out of your life, I will sit here quietly and leave you to yourself in London. I even promise to get you a separate suite if that's what you want, and before you sputter at me about cost, no matter what, I'll still cover the bill since I was the one who changed your plans."

He swallowed, and Maggie could see a flash of nerves in his eyes. "When we broke up last fall, I honestly thought it was over. I was so angry with you; I figured it was for the best. I even came back to Boston planning to start dating as soon as possible. I was going to prove to myself—and you— that I could go on. Then I came back from Ireland and heard Devon's voice on my machine talking about Jake's death, and something changed. All I could think about was how upset you, Eli, and Nicky must have been. I kept seeing their faces the night he showed up – I've never seen love so evident."

He stopped for a moment, searching how to make her understand. "I would wake up in the middle of the night, reaching for you, wanting to take the hurt away. Even though you hung up on me that day, I kept thinking about you. Then I met Alexis, and we started going out fairly regularly, but it didn't feel right – I mean, in some ways, it was a perfect match, but it left me cold. I started seeing a therapist, trying to figure out what the hell was wrong with me, and trying to figure out why kids scare me so much. Maybe I was trying to prove to my therapist I was over you, so I tried harder with Lexi. I thought it might work, or at least, I could make it work with enough effort. Then when I saw you today, it was all so fucking clear."

Cupping her face with his hands, he lifted her head. "Look at me, Maggie." She resentfully made eye contact. "I love you and I probably should have confessed that a long time ago. I love you with all my heart. And not just you; somewhere along the way, I grew to love Eli and Nicky. When we broke up, I mourned losing you but also missed the everyday contact with *them*. I know it won't be easy, but I'm willing to do whatever I need to make it work. More therapy, whatever. I want to be with all of you, whether it's in London or Vermont."

This was all too much for Maggie. "You love me?" Her brow furrowed. "You're sitting there saying you *love* me, when not twelve hours ago you were eating lunch with a woman you referred to as 'a sure thing.'"

Andre shifted uncomfortably. "I know, but I was so annoyed by your attitude, I would have done anything to get your attention. I know that sounds immature, but when you made eye contact with me and then looked away, I was ready to punch someone." He squeezed her hand. "I'm so sorry for saying that. Maggie, I don't really know if she was a sure thing. We went out to dinners and movies; nothing more."

"You didn't sleep with her?"

"I didn't sleep with her." He gave a sexy grin. "You ruined me for other women, Mags. After you, anyone would be a step down."

Maggie ignored his comment. "So how could you go from her to me in less than twelve hours?"

"I know it sounds insane. Truly, I do. Before I saw you in Quincy Market, I was trying to figure out why it felt wrong being with her. Then I saw you and you were ready to kill me. At that moment, I should've cared how Lexi would feel, but all that mattered was *you*. As I walked toward you, all I cared about was how to make it work – and what you would do if I grabbed you and kissed you senseless. Then you dropped your London bombshell and when you walked away, I understood."

"What? What did you understand?"

"That nothing mattered but *us*. That you're Eli and Nicky's mom and that's part of the reason I love you – your love for them is so strong you would walk through fire for them."

All of this sounded nice, but in Maggie's mind, it didn't change much. "But you don't want to be a father. Now that Jake's gone, they need me more than ever and they can't handle a part-time, half-hearted man in their lives."

He corrected her gently. "They need *us*. They need two parents who are madly in love, who love them. That night we broke up, you were right; I did have fun with the boys. Part of the reason it was fun was because you stopped worrying so much and let me be part of the family. Before that night, you would've slit your own throat before you asked me to help with the boys. That night, you let me into your world, and I loved it. But Mags, I want it all with you. I want to be part of the good, the bad, and the mundane. I don't want to sit on the sidelines."

Maggie's eyes filled with tears. "Andre, this is too much. You've gone from not wanting children at all, to claiming you do – I'm absolutely overwhelmed by this." Her voice broke. "I don't know what to say."

For a moment, frustration washed over Andre. Couldn't anything be simple with Maggie? Searching for a way to make her understand, he had to ask the question foremost on his mind. "Do you love me?"

Her answer was swift. "Oh, God, *yes*. I love you completely and I have for ages. "

He leaned forward smiling. "Then the rest will work out. I love you, you love me, and we can figure things out as we go."

A glimmer of hope ran through Maggie. "Do you mean it?"

"With all my heart. Do you?"

Her kiss was all the answer he needed.

The rest of the flight was pure magic. Sipping champagne, they planned their time in London and talked about the months they were apart. Several hours into the flight, Maggie's eyes began to droop.

Andre put his arm around her. "Go to sleep, my Magdalena. I'll be your pillow."

It sounded so good, but Maggie hesitated. "That won't be comfortable for you."

"Yes, it will. Just having you back makes anything feel good. Now rest, so you'll be wide awake later in London."

Maggie gave a sleepy but sexy smile. "Why? You have plans later on?"

"Magdalena, I plan to make up for lost months…"

With that, Maggie snuggled into his arms, dreaming of what was to come later.

After clearing customs, Andre guided Maggie to the front entrance. Still sleepy, Maggie looked in vain for her hotel's van. Andre looked amused. "Maggie, what are you doing?"

"Looking for the hotel van."

"Darling, I changed your hotel reservation, remember?" He motioned toward a black limousine parked at the curb. "That's our ride."

Feeling like a child, Maggie giggled. "No way! Andre, what were you thinking? I don't need a limo."

"Well, I wasn't sure how hard I needed to work to convince you to take me back."

"Maybe I should've played harder to get."

He chuckled. "Get in the car."

In the hotel elevator, Maggie tiredly rubbed her eyes. "Maybe I should've slept last night in the hotel, instead of pacing."

"Why were you pacing?"

"I hate when the boys fly without me, so I was worried until my mom called and then I kept thinking about you. I sat at the window, looking out, wondering what you were doing, and hoping that… I don't know, maybe I was hoping I'd run into you, and maybe I was hoping I wouldn't."

"Are you sorry that you did?"

She squeezed his hand. "How could I be sorry? If I hadn't, you wouldn't be here now."

At the door to the suite, Andre hesitated. "I booked only one suite, hoping I could convince you to hear me out, but I understand if you need your own space. It's up to you."

Maggie wasn't sure what he meant. "Are you asking me to stay with you? Or asking me to stay in the other bedroom?"

"My love, I am trying to be considerate that a lot has changed in the last few hours, and I want to give you exactly what you need."

"Oh." Joy welled up. "I need you. I don't need another room, or suite. I want to be with *you*."

He kissed her deeply, then opened the door. "That's what I was hoping you'd say…"

Chapter Thirty-Six

Maggie awoke the next morning, encircled in Andre's arms, her head resting on his wide chest, his heart beating steadily under her ear. A satisfied smile spread across her face when she remembered the night before.

"What are you smiling about? You look like the Cheshire cat."

Maggie looked up to find Andre's eyes on her. She blushed. "I was just thinking about last night."

Andre rolled onto his side and gazed at her lovingly. "Which part? The absolute mind-altering passion? The freedom to finally admit we love each other? Or was it the room-service picnic early this morning?"

"The picnic. Definitely thinking about the *picnic*," she teased.

Swiftly, Andre pinned her beneath him, his need for her clearly evident. "Love, if all you can think about is that *picnic*, I have to try harder to be memorable."

She giggled. "I can't wait—"

Hours later, Maggie put on her sunglasses as they exited the hotel. Holding her hand, Andre gestured down the street. "Where do you want to go?"

"Andre, I'm a woman and I'm less than a block away from Harrods. I'm going there to spend obscene amounts of money."

Andre watched in amusement as Maggie charged through the store, looking every bit the urban professional woman in her beige jacket, smart skirt, and heels. Laden with gifts for the boys, she grinned at Andre. "One more department? Please?"

"Your wish is my command. Where to?"

"The china department. I want to get my parents an anniversary gift."

Once there, Andre thankfully sank onto a plush chair. How did Maggie manage to keep walking and shopping, all the time wearing heels? Watching her from across the room, he saw her looking at a set of wine glasses. Picking up the bags, he walked over. "Do you like those for your parents?"

"Aren't they beautiful?" The fine crystal was etched with a delicate thistle design.

"They're gorgeous."

She put them back on the shelf. "They really aren't my parents' style. I guess I'll get them the candlesticks instead."

As Maggie paid, her gaze kept returning to the glasses, almost wistfully.

After a leisurely lunch, Maggie and Andre wandered through the park. Suddenly, Maggie seemed to pick up speed.

Even with his long legs, Andre needed to hurry to keep up. "Maggie, what are you doing? You're almost running."

Her eyes were clear and excited. "I remember where we are. We're almost at the Albert Memorial."

Her comment surprised him. "I didn't know you'd been here before."

Maggie shrugged. "We came here when I was really little; probably about five. My dad was stationed in Germany at the time, and we flew here from the states to meet him for a vacation. I don't remember much, except my mom brought me to see the memorial." She paused,

"It was one of the few things I ever did with my mom alone. We came to see it, just the two of us."

As it came into view, Maggie's eyes filled with tears. "It's just as I remembered it. I've never seen anything this perfect. I remember my mom telling me it was a monument to commemorate love. I always thought that was such a beautiful idea."

Andre pulled her close, kissing her passionately. "It is beautiful, almost as beautiful as you. I love you."

She leaned against him, hugging him tightly. "I love you, too."

That afternoon, Maggie seemed quiet, almost distracted.

Andre looked over at her. "Maggie, are you okay? You've gotten really quiet."

She nodded. "I'm fine. Just thinking."

"Do you want to talk about it?"

"No, just getting ready for the meeting tomorrow. I need to gather my thoughts."

That evening, she organized herself for the school meeting scheduled for the next morning.

Andre lay on the bed watching her. "Are you sure you don't want me to go with you?"

Maggie leaned down to kiss his cheek. "Thank you, but no. I need to do this alone. Then I'll come back here and tell you all about it." She pulled a folder from her bag. "You don't mind, do you?"

Deep down, Andre admitted he was frustrated, but it was her decision. "No, I understand."

"Thank you. What are you going to do while I'm gone?"

"I'll probably call the office, do a bit of work, run an errand or two, and maybe check out a museum."

"Okay. Do you want to meet here after, or meet somewhere for dinner?"

Andre pulled her down onto the bed, his hands strong and warm as they slid under her robe. "Meet me here. And then we'll see…"

The next night, Andre opened the door to the suite. Maggie's coat was flung over a chair. "Maggie? I'm back. How was your day?"

His throat tightened as she opened the bathroom door, wearing a simple dark rose dress that swirled around her ankles. The soft sound of tinkling bells sounded as she stepped toward him in her high heels, and Andre glimpsed a delicate silver chain around her ankle.

He leaned down to kiss her cheek lightly. His senses awakened as he caught the scent of Chanel No. 5, and something more, something simply Maggie. "Hi."

She hesitated for just a moment before smiling as she took in every detail of his blazer and perfectly pressed pants, seeing how the ivory shirt highlighted his darker skin tone. "Hi."

"You're beautiful." Andre looked uncomfortable for a moment. "I meant to say you look especially beautiful tonight." His smile broadened as he stroked her cheek lightly with his index finger and she shivered with pleasure. He tried not to notice her nipples tightening under the thin fabric of her dress but couldn't repress his body's immediate reaction. "No, I was right the first time. You're beautiful. Period."

Maggie's face burned. "Thank you. So are you. I mean, you look gorgeous yourself." Taking his hand, she shook her head. "No more. Let's talk about something else before I sound like even more of an idiot."

Andre squeezed her hand. "Ready to go? Do you still want to go out, or are you too tired?"

"I'm ready. I spent the whole day waiting to be with

you. Just let me grab my purse and we can go."

In the elevator, Maggie squeezed Andre's arm, enjoying his solid presence beside her. "How was your day?"

"My day was fine. That is, it was bearable except that I had to spend the entire day without you, hanging out in stores and museums." His eyes crinkled at the corners. "I spent every moment missing you, wondering how you were, and trying to guess what was going on at the school. Each moment I wasn't with you, was..." he leaned closer to whisper in her ear, "one moment when I wasn't doing this."

Maggie's heart raced as he pulled her toward him and pressed his mouth to hers. His hand was warm on her back. Unconsciously, she moved closer, tipping her head slightly, her fingers grasping the lapel of his suit coat as his tongue slipped into her mouth...

When the elevator stopped, they pulled apart guiltily, and she quickly moved to stand just in front of him, her hands brushing distractedly at the front of her skirt.

A group of laughing senior citizens crowded onto the elevator. Seeing the color on Maggie's cheekbones, one man winked knowingly at Andre. Andre grinned back conspiratorially and leaned down to kiss Maggie's ear lightly. Her soft gasp was all the invitation he needed to wrap his arms around her. She leaned back against him, wishing the elevator hadn't stopped at all.

Chapter Thirty-Seven

The cab whisked them by the brightly lit Buckingham Palace, slowing just long enough for them to admire the unicorn gates.

Minutes later, Maggie looked confused as they pulled up in front of an antiqued sign of a swan. "How did you pick this place?"

He shrugged. "When I used to frequent London, I'd come here for the fish and chips and cold beer. You mentioned last night you wanted fish and chips tonight."

Maggie stretched up to kiss him fully. "You're always so thoughtful, thank you. And thank you for being so understanding about today."

With loaded plates, they found seats at the picnic tables clustered near the sidewalk. After a few bites,

Andre put his fork down. "Are you going to tell me about today?"

Maggie chewed a mouthful and swallowed. "It went well – really well."

His tone was neutral. "I would've thought if it went so well your tone would be more enthusiastic."

She sighed. "I know. I think I'm just overwhelmed. It seems almost too good to be true. Now I'm torn."

"Torn how?"

Her words came out in a rush. "I don't know. It seems like such a wonderful opportunity, but what will happen back at home? Will I still like that job if I go back to it in a year? Would the boys like it here? What if I got here and didn't like it? What would it do to *us*?"

Andre chose his words carefully. "Maggie, ultimately, you need to make this decision based on what feels right to you. We'll make it work no matter where you are. If you're here, I'll try to be here as much as possible, and if you're back in Vermont, I'll be there when I can."

A sense of relief washed over her. "Really?"

"Really." He smiled. "Now tell me about the school."

Back at the hotel, Andre showered while Maggie called Kim.

"Hello."

"Hey, it's me."

"How the hell are you? How was the interview? Are you really there with Andre? Why the hell didn't you call me sooner? You sent me one lousy email, with no juicy details."

Maggie laughed. "Damn, what did you want me to do – call you in the middle of sex?"

"A guy dashes onto a plane to be with you. He flies across the Atlantic to convince you to take him back, and you can't even bother to call your own sister?"

"Sorry. I'm sorry. Hey, Kim, listen to me, I have to talk fast because Andre will be out of the shower soon."

Kim's tone immediately got serious. "Go ahead."

"I'm wigging out. I'm here with the man of my dreams, who now wants to be a father, I've been offered a kick-ass job here, and I'm losing my fucking mind."

"Huh?"

"I can't take this. I don't know what to do. Do I take the job? Is this what I want to do forever, you know, work in a school? If I *do* want to teach for the foreseeable future, this job is a huge step up, but if I take the job, what will that do to my relationship with Andre? What will that relationship do to the boys? I mean, he says he thinks he loves the boys, but what if he doesn't? Is this going to fuck them up? They certainly don't need any more separation issues. What the hell do I do?"

"Deep breath, Mags."

"I can't take a deep breath. I don't know what to do! I can hear Mom bitching how bad all these changes would be for the boys." Maggie heard Andre opening the bathroom door. "I have to go. Love you."

"Maggie, wait!"

"Bye, Kim."

Chapter Thirty-Eight

That night, and the long day after, Andre tried hard to pretend he didn't notice Maggie's increasing withdrawal. Every time he touched her or asked her a question, she jumped. Finally, he snapped. "We need to talk."

Sitting on the couch, Maggie feigned ignorance. "About what?"

Andre sat down on the coffee table, forcing Maggie to look at him. "About us. About what the hell is going on here."

"I don't know what you mean."

Andre's anger surprised him. "Maggie, you're here with me, but you're not. Ever since you went to see the

265

school, it's like I'm not here. You're so far inside your own head, I might as well leave."

"I'm here! Who the hell do you think has been with you day and night?"

"Yes, physically, you're here, but…you're not *here*. I don't know if it's because you don't know what to do about the job, or something else, like us, but you are completely shutting me out. Something is ripping you apart inside, and all you talk about is the weather and the soccer game on television. I don't give a fuck about either; all I care about is what's going on with you."

Maggie felt tears pooling in her eyes, knowing he was right. "I'm not meaning to. I don't know what to do. I feel like I have way too many important things to decide right now, and I don't have the foggiest fucking idea what to do."

"Like what? Talk to me, Maggie, please." He held her hands tightly. "You're keeping things from me, and I don't know what you're thinking or feeling. All I know is that if this is the way our relationship is going to be, then it isn't really a relationship."

Maggie felt panic forming. "What are you saying?"

"I'm saying you need to either be with me with your whole heart or not at all. I'm not settling for part way. You need to trust me with both you and the boys. You need to let me share your burdens, trusting I will still love you no matter what. At the risk of giving you an ultimatum, I need to know once and for all if you're willing to try, because I can't stand being here, feeling like you already left me."

Maggie stood up, needing air before she suffocated. "I need to go for a walk. Alone."

Andre fought the urge to shake her or take her to bed, hoping to break through the walls she was building between them. He took a steadying breath. "Take your cell phone, please."

"Okay."

"I'm here if you need me." His voice softened. "I love you."

Maggie stopped, resting her hand on the doorknob. "I know you do, and no matter what, that helps."

Walking out of the hotel, Maggie automatically started through the park. The school children ran shouting down the walkways, enjoying the afternoon sun. She walked and walked, not paying attention to where she was going, trying to quiet the clamoring voices in her mind. Exhausted, she dropped onto a nearby bench. Staring blindly ahead, she fought the urge to cry.

The cell phone chirped shrilly. Pulling it out nervously from her pocket, she answered. "Hello?"

"Magdalena?"

Just hearing her mother's voice made Maggie's heart race in fear. *Damn!* This was not what she needed right now. "Are the boys okay? What's wrong?"

"Nothing's wrong with the boys. They're just fine. They're sleeping like angels. I just spoke with Kimberly and clearly, I need to talk to *you*."

Shit. Here comes the lecture. "I can explain, Mom."

Her mother's voice was gentler than normal, "Explain what? That you're confused and afraid?"

Maggie was shocked, "Huh?"

"Listen to me, Magdalena. I understand how you feel right now, and I know about Andre. Kim says we'll like him."

"Oh."

"Yes, oh. Aside from my wishing you would go to church more often to ask God for help, I'm not worried about what you're doing with Andre. But sweetie, you need to make the right decisions about all of this."

Maggie's voice rose defensively, "I'm trying to!"

"I know you're trying, but making the right decision may not come easy to you." Her voice softened. "Maggie, you know we loved Jake."

"How could I miss it, Mom? You made sure I knew how unhappy you were about the divorce."

"I know, and I shouldn't have. We loved Jake, but he was a horrible husband, and not because he was a soldier or because he was away a lot. Your father was gone as much as Jake, but he never strayed. I should never have insinuated you could have tried harder, that was not fair, and it wasn't supportive. Kim says Andre won't ever treat you that way. Eli says Andre is kind to you and even helps with the dishes. Jake never did dishes, and God knows you could use help in the kitchen."

"Mom! Is there a point here?"

"Don't get snippy. There *is* a point. Andre is the man of your destiny. You've been dancing back and forth with him for a while. Now, if you truly love him, you need to commit to making this work."

"I'm trying."

"No, darling, I'm not sure you are, and I think I know why."

"Why?"

"Kim says you're all aflutter about the job and Andre, and you can't make a decision on either. Part of your hesitation right now is because Andre may join your life for good; you never had a man like that before. You married a soldier; he wasn't always around, so you don't know how to be married full-time. As for the children, you really ruled the roost, and the boys needed you most. Just like you children needed me." Maggie heard the smile in her voice. "Then, when your father would come home, he was the hero. I was the peanut butter sandwich in your lives, and he was the chocolate cake. I loved having him home, but it always hurt when you all wanted *him* to read to you instead of me."

"But Mom…"

"But nothing. You need to give priority to love. Figure things out with Andre."

Tears slowly ran down Maggie's cheeks. "Mom, I don't know how."

"Do you love him enough to work at this?"

"Yes. Oh, Mom, I love him so much."

"Then get off your behind and do what it takes."

"Okay, Mom." Maggie swallowed hard, overwhelmed by her love for her mother. "I love you, Mom."

"I know you do, and I love you. Maggie. You are a wonderful mother and daughter, and you were a great wife. I don't tell you enough how very proud I am of you, probably because I know you're so strong you don't need my praise."

"Yes, I do, Mom. It means a lot to me."

"Then hear me clearly, Magdalena, I love you, and I am very proud of you. You are an amazing daughter, mother, sister, educator, and you were an amazing wife.

Maybe this time your man will treat you the right way, the way you deserve."

"Do you really think so?"

"I do. Now, go find your destiny. I suspect it's waiting closer than you think."

Maggie hung up, wiping her eyes. Then she looked around, trying to get her bearings. Across the walkway was a map.

She walked to it quickly, pinpointing the hotel. If she walked straight through the park, she would be back at the hotel shortly.

Maggie strode down the path, oblivious to the children and flowers, her mind focusing on Andre. Suddenly, gold spires came into view, and then all of the Albert Memorial glittered before her.

As she came closer, she glimpsed a familiar figure sitting on the bench, watching the walkway carefully. She ran.

Andre stood, bracing himself. By the time she reached him, tears were flowing down her cheeks. Throwing her arms around his neck, she hugged him with all her love and strength. "I love you. It's you that matters. You and I being together matters – not a job."

Andre held her close, wiping away the tears. "I love you, too. Of course, we matter."

Maggie pulled him down to sit next to her on the bench. "I talked with my mom, and I figured it out. I was so busy flipping out about the job and you and how to make it all work, and how the boys would feel, oh, and so much other shit, I lost sight of the fact I love you, and that the love between us and our love for the boys is most important." She smiled. "And that was a really long sentence, but I needed to tell you."

He chuckled. "I'm glad you did."

Maggie narrowed her eyes. "How did you know I'd come by here?"

"I figured you'd head into the park. Then I figured if you worked it out, you'd probably head back to the hotel by this route."

"I'm so glad you're here! I thought I'd have to go all the way back to the hotel. Then I was worried you wouldn't be there, and I needed to tell you I love you, now and forever."

Andre stroked her cheek. "And I love you." He pulled a bag from beside the bench. "This is for you."

"You got me a present after I was such a bitch?"

"You weren't a bitch." Maggie raised an eyebrow. "Well, maybe a bit bitchy, but you just needed to figure it all out. Open the box."

Maggie carefully opened the wrapping paper. Nestled inside was a box from the china department at

Harrods. Maggie held her breath as she opened the box, her eyes widening with joy when she found two crystal glasses, the ones she had so loved in the store. "Oh, Andre. They're beautiful. Thank you." She bit her lower lip, her eyes shining. "Thank you so much."

Andre put the box on the bench between them and took her hand. "I thought they could be *our* glasses, for our special celebrations."

Maggie touched one glass reverently, tracing the stem of the flower. "What a beautiful idea. Maybe we could use them tonight."

"Maybe we could. But we need to settle one more thing."

"What?"

Andre reached inside his blazer and pulled a small green box from inside. "Magdalena Carlota Erickson O'Brien, will you marry me? Will you let me be your husband, your lover, your best friend, the father of your sons, and hopefully, maybe the father of your future children?" He opened the box, and a beautiful diamond ring nestled inside threw flashes of light.

A smile spread across Maggie's face as she realized her destiny had arrived. As she looked over Andre's shoulder at the monument, everything made sense. She leaned forward, her lips almost touching his. "I would love to marry you. Today, tomorrow, whenever, I can't wait to marry you, Andre. To have you be my husband, my lover, and the father of *all* my children."

And then she kissed him.

Epilogue

Fifteen months later, Andre carried the bags of groceries in from the car, Eli running up the steps to hold the screen door open for him. "Thanks, Eli."

"You're welcome, Daddy." Following Andre down the hall, "Daddy, once we put away the groceries, do you want to go for a swim?"

Andre looked down at his stepson, feeling his heart swell with love for the little boy who so wholeheartedly accepted him into his life. "Of course, I do, buddy. Let's put away the groceries, then see how Mommy's doing."

At that moment, Maggie came into the room. Andre had to smile watching her bend with her very pregnant body to hug Eli. "Hey, dude, how was soccer?"

"It was great! Daddy even got to see the scrimmage."

Maggie smiled at Andre over Eli's head. "He did?"

"And we're going swimming in a bit. Do you want to go?"

"No sweetie, but I'd love to sit on the deck and watch you guys swim. Nick should be back in a few minutes; he just went to walk the dog with Uncle Mike."

Minutes later, Eli ran upstairs to get his bathing suit, and Andre came over to smile down at his wife. He kissed her tenderly, "Missed you."

"Missed you, too."

"How's the munchkin?" he asked, gently rubbing her swollen abdomen, feeling the baby turn as he touched her.

"Busy," she yawned, "really, really busy."

Andre swept her into his arms, "Then let's get you settled and off your feet, Mrs. Serapes."

Maggie kissed him, a wave of desire hitting her immediately, as it did every time they kissed. "Too bad we can't take a nap together..."

He placed her gently in a chaise on the deck, then bent over her, "Tonight, I promise." He stroked her cheek, "Even though I'm still not convinced we should at this point in the pregnancy."

"You heard the doctor; it's fine."

Three days later, Andre walked the two boys over to Mike's house, the two of them chattering, "So the baby is really coming today, Daddy, really?"

Holding both their hands, Andre smiled down at Nick, who asked the question so seriously. "Today, Nick. Tomorrow at the latest. You officially won't be the youngest one in the family anymore."

At the front door, Mike was waiting for them. "Hey guys, come on in. We'll hang out here, then go swimming, eat dinner, and when the baby is here, we'll go visit at the hospital."

After kissing the boys goodbye, Andre turned back toward the house. Just then, he heard a small voice, "Daddy?"

Andre turned around to see Eli looking at him with fear in his eyes. "Daddy, Mommy is going to be okay, right? She's not going to die, is she?"

Even though he knew he needed to get back to take Maggie to the hospital, Andre turned back to pick Eli up in his arms, feeling little hands wrap around his neck tightly. Suddenly, the boy began to cry. "Daddy, I'm so scared. I don't want her to die too."

Andre searched for the words that would soothe him. "Eli, Mommy is going to be fine. She's healthy, the baby is healthy, and the hospital is great. I'll take Mommy to the hospital, and as soon as the baby is here, I'll call Uncle Mike to bring you to us. I promise it's going to be okay." He kissed his hair. "Okay now, it's your job to take care of Nicky. Remember, I love you."

"Love you too, Daddy."

Ten hours later, Andre carefully handed a small baby girl to a very tired but happy Maggie. "Here she is, Mags. Our daughter."

"Our daughter." Maggie looked up at Andre. "I love you."

Andre lay down beside Maggie, one arm around his wife, the other protectively over their newborn daughter, feeling a rush of love stronger than any he felt before. "I love you too, both of you." He kissed Maggie gently. "I love all of you, our perfect family."

Just then, they heard small feet patter in the hallway, and Andre smiled. "I think we have visitors."

Nick and Eli rushed into the room, followed by an amused Mike, Devon, Claire, and Kim. Andre slid to the side a bit, smiling at his sons. "Guys, come on up with Mommy and me. Meet your sister."

Acknowledgements

Thanks to Between the Lines Publishing for their belief in my stories. Thanks to Cyn, Sutton, and Penny for their amazing editorial support.

Thanks to Ben, who picks up the slack when I'm in a writing frenzy, and to Lou, Scout, and Hattie for keeping me company while I type away on my laptop.

Kris is an educator, award winning screenwriter, author, and ghostwriter who lives on a small family farm in Central Vermont with her husband and youngest son. When not writing, she enjoys time with her husband, children, and grandchildren, traveling, gardening, cheering for the Red Sox, and taking care of her dogs, cat, sheep, bees and chickens. Kris is also an avid knitter and spinner, and often her best ideas for novels come when at the spinning wheel or in the garden.